Week at the Nees'

VOLUME ONE IN THE MARCUS NEE SERIES

RONAN JOYCE

For my old friend, Simon W. Johnstone (1948-2009), without whom this book would not have been written. And for Ian Shuttleworth, who inspired me by maintaining his grace and dignity under horrifying conditions.

MONDAY

1

MARCUS Nee stood on the edge of the cliff near his farm and watched in silent anticipation as Judas tried in vain to move his bowels. Unaccustomed as he was to seeing the black and white border collie in such a compromising position, Marcus was reluctant to look away. He was glad of the distraction; anything to take his mind off the pile of potatoes waiting for him in the farmyard below.

His companion since childhood, Judas had all the characteristics Marcus recognised in himself: he was disobedient, had a healthy disregard for authority and was allergic to gluten, to the point of constipation. Despite their apparent lack of affection for one another, they were seldom apart. In the years they had been together, Marcus could find no practical use for the brute and considered him more trouble than he was worth. He sighed as the beast suspended his efforts, scurrying off to find a more secluded location to do his business.

'Ah well, better luck next time. I told you not to eat all that bread.'

Marcus turned towards the sea and watched the waves pounding into the rocks below. Raising his chipped ceramic mug to his lips, he took a mouthful of tea and admired the tremendous span of the Atlantic Ocean. In the distance, he spotted Willie's yacht bouncing across the water, its white sails bulging in the wind. Right on schedule, he thought, looking at his watch. He wondered how many bottles of poteen his friend had sold and what news he would bring from the mainland.

He tried to imagine what the view must have been like more than four hundred years before as the Spanish Armada scuttled homeward with its weary sailors throwing cannon and horses overboard as they went. He could almost see the mighty galleons with their tattered sails as they crashed into the Irish coast.

When the wind picked up, Marcus bowed his head to protect his eyes. He turned around and made his way back to the farmyard to finish his work and check on the old man.

It would be a gross understatement to say that Marcus disliked cutting potatoes. But it had to be done—they were the main ingredient in his poteen, and they were cheap and plentiful. There was no getting around the fact that they had to be cut and mashed to facilitate the distilling process. It was the price of doing business and, in the scheme of things, it was a small price to pay. It weighed heavily on his mind that he had to break the law to make the money he needed. He considered some of the other illegal activities he could have pursued and, as nefarious enterprises went, distilling poteen was the safest option. Robbing a bank would take too much planning and there was also the chance he could get shot. Kidnapping a wealthy business tycoon would be too messy, especially considering his disproportionate guilt complex. All things considered, poteen was the best option, even if he disliked the process.

In the distance, he could see his father, Eamon, sitting on a gate, dangling his foot against the rusted metal. Marcus had no idea what the future held for the pair of them, but he hoped it had nothing to do with potatoes. As he neared the stone wall that marked the edge of his farm, Judas appeared out of nowhere and darted between his legs, nearly tripping him. Marcus cursed as he broke into a run and jumped the stone wall. Clearing it with inches to spare, he landed on a mound of soft hay on the other side and was careful not to break his ceramic mug. Standing up, he brushed the hay off his clothes and ran his fingers through his thatch of thick brown hair. He caught himself admiring his reflection in the discarded windscreen of an old tractor. *Not bad looking for a man of forty*, he thought to himself. His nose and mouth were smaller than normal, but his chin was prominent enough to tie the rest of his face together with a distinguished flourish. In contrast to the rocky fields of Inis Mór, he had an air of congeniality and purpose.

When he reached the middle of the yard, he sat down on the three-legged milking stool and returned to the task at hand.

Cutting potatoes in cold weather was a tricky proposition, as Marcus discovered once when he almost lost his fingers. A decent pair of rubber gloves and a sharp knife were definite requirements. It was also important to make sure the potatoes were clean, so they didn't subvert the distilling process.

Conditions at the farmyard were far from ideal but Marcus had streamlined the process to reduce the amount of heavy lifting involved. To save himself from lugging heavy sacks of potatoes from the kitchen all day, he set up his enterprise in the farmyard so that Shergar could do all the work. Marcus was sure the old nag would have preferred to spend his days frolicking in the fields, and he didn't blame him. But if he wanted to be fed and watered every day, he had to do some work.

Marcus had already been through at least three hundred potatoes and his hands were almost frozen solid. The wind coming in from the Atlantic was as cold as he had ever experienced.

Nearly finished, he promised himself, *just a few more to go.*

'You better stay on your toes,' Eamon shouted. 'I heard Lucy is back.'

Marcus remained silent, unwilling to involve his father in a topic that had been causing him several sleepless nights lately. He couldn't think about Lucy now—he was struggling to grip the knife with his frigid hands.

'It'll be pissing down soon,' said the old man, shifting on the gate and losing his balance. He righted himself just in time but couldn't prevent his bottle of poteen from landing on a fresh pile of horseshit.

Marcus looked up at the sky and then checked his watch. 'You're joking,' he told his father. 'There isn't a cloud in the sky. Are you making a weather forecast or a philosophical observation?'

Eamon growled as he repositioned himself on his wrought-iron perch. 'Get that bottle for me, will you, like a good man?'

Marcus ignored his father and was annoyed the old man had nothing better to do at that hour of the morning. Just because he was elderly and handicapped didn't mean he could lounge around all day drinking.

'There are eight hundred people who live on this bloody island and you're the only one who doesn't do any work.'

'Can't you see I'm disabled?'

Once a tall, elegant man, Eamon had become withered and scrawny in old age. Even so, he had lost none of his poise and his cold blue eyes seemed to mellow when he smiled. He was proud of the fact that his teeth were his own—though he was missing a few at the front, which allowed him to affect a ghastly sneer when the situation required it. He always wore a tweed cap with a matching jacket and a single wellington boot with the top turned down.

Eamon had lost his right leg in a farm accident a few years previously. He had a perfectly good prosthetic limb, but he preferred not to wear it around the farm, thus underscoring his inability to work.

Marcus looked at his watch again. He was behind schedule—he'd only just finished cutting the spuds. His fingers had had enough, though, so he rose from his stool and rinsed his hands in a bucket of water. He dried them on a towel and put on his warm leather gloves.

'His lordship will be here soon,' said Marcus, walking over to his father. He picked up the bottle of poteen, taking extra care not to get any excrement on his gloves, and handed it to the old man. 'Why don't you make yourself useful and put the kettle on?'

Ever since Eamon's accident, Marcus had had the unenviable tasks of looking after his father and managing the farm. There was a limit to what Eamon could do around the place, but there seemed to be no limit to the damage he could cause, both to himself and to the farm. Marcus didn't mind putting his life on hold to look after the old man. His father raised him after his mother died, so he owed him a great deal.

The old bugger had farmed these fields of useless muck and stones near Cockle Strand for more years than he could remember. And his father before him had done the same. Marcus inherited the land after the old man's accident—or at least he inherited the work. His only saving grace was that he had found a better use for the land than his father and his father before him. He discovered he could make more money using the potatoes to distill illegal poteen than selling them at the market.

'Make your own bloody tea,' Eamon shouted as Marcus climbed over the wall at the end of the yard and untied Shergar. He backed the animal towards a two-wheeled cart that was already loaded with bags of cut potatoes. After a few failed attempts, Marcus managed to raise the cart to the proper height and attach it to the horse's harness. He made sure all the straps were tight, and then he slapped the animal on the rump.

The Nees used to own two horses, but one of them had died mysteriously. Marcus didn't know it for a fact, but he suspected the poor creature had downed some poteen that his drunken father had left in the yard. Now he'd have to get another beast at the Maam Cross Fair—when he could scrape the money together.

'That's all the booze you're getting now, so make it last,' he said to Eamon, who was still sitting on the gate.

One of the measures Marcus had to implement while caring for his father was a restriction on the amount of poteen the old man was allowed to consume. Just because they had a steady supply of the illegal brew didn't mean Eamon could help himself to what he liked. He was allowed half a pint daily for medicinal purposes and the rest was kept under lock and key. The owners of the island's pubs and shops were also under strict instructions not to serve the old man.

As he guided Shergar over to the beach, Marcus allowed himself a smile at the thought of his one-legged father hopping through horseshit to get back to the house.

As Marcus and Judas made their way across the muddy fields to the inlet, he cursed the weather and pulled the lapel of his overcoat up over his ears. At least it's not raining, he thought. Inis Mór was a desolate place during the winter months. The treeless landscape provided hardly any shelter from the savage ocean winds and the barren limestone fields provided little sustenance for the farmers who laboured in appalling conditions.

But it was beautiful, too. The craggy landscape and the sheer cliffs were known throughout the world for their magnificence. The grey-purple sky seemed to intensify the colours of the island, the fields of green and the thatch-roofed cottages of stone.

Marcus loved Inis Mór and he took his duties and commitments seriously. He thrived on the tranquillity and the long summer days when nature was in full bloom. And then there was always the important task of catching up with the latest gossip at the local pub. He lived for the days spent fishing at Serpent Hole, playing Gaelic football on the beach or rowing his *currach* for hours around the island.

Thanks to his rowing, he was much fitter than would normally be expected of a man of his age. Like most of the islanders, Marcus had learned to row at an early age.

When he studied for his Leaving Certificate with the Jesuits in Galway, he represented the school at several international regattas. He did the same when he studied at Trinity College in Dublin. He competed at dozens of *currach*-rowing festivals around Galway Bay and across the country, including the world-famous *Cruinniu na mBad* Festival in Kinvara. He still holds the record for being the fastest person to row the thirty-five kilometres from Inis Mór to the mainland.

Marcus raised his head when he reached the inlet and spotted the white sails in the distance. He looked south and could clearly make out the islands of Inis Meáin and Inis Oírr sprawled out across the ocean. Judas barked as he ran ahead of his master towards the shore. Willie's yacht provided a wonderful spectacle, rising and falling over the waves as it neared the beach. Marcus watched as his friend dropped anchor, jumped onto the little jetty and made his way onto the beach.

'How's it going, your lordship?'

William Shuttleworth-Banks wasn't a lord, but Marcus liked to tease him about his posh English accent. Just because they were firm friends didn't mean he could be forgiven for being English.

'Nice weather for it, my boy,' Willie lied, rubbing his hands against the cold.

'So, how's business?' Marcus asked.

'Not bad at all, dear boy.' Willie reached into his pocket to take out a wad of cash. 'Sold the whole lot this trip.'

'Things are picking up then?'

Marcus accepted the notes and smiled. He was curious about the sales aspect of the business, but he knew Willie would never divulge his contacts or say where he sold his poteen.

'At any given time, there's a party going on somewhere in Ireland.' Willie leaned on his yacht and admired the limestone contours of Aran. 'You just have to follow the sound of the music, dear boy.'

Marcus and Willie had built their little poteen business into a lucrative venture. They had only one pot still but the overheads were low and they were making plenty of cash. Marcus grew the potatoes, they distilled the liquor in a shed at the back of Willie's home and they used Willie's yacht to distribute the finished product.

While Marcus knew his friend had recently shown signs of restlessness and suspected he wanted to pack it in, he hadn't considered the consequences of this. The business had been good to them but it wasn't easy money. They had to work hard for their ill-gotten gains and they had plenty of competition. Like any business, they had to keep their customers happy with a quality product and reliable deliveries. But it wasn't a young man's game and Marcus was mindful of the fact that Willie was getting on in years.

Willie grabbed hold of Shergar and guided the spud-laden animal towards the water's edge. He stopped for a moment and placed his hands on his hips, palms down with his thumbs pointing forward, as if to straighten his body to relieve a backache.

'You don't look so good,' said Marcus. 'Are you feeling okay?'

'Just a touch of the gout, dear boy.'

Marcus looked at his friend. 'I heard Lucy was back and trying to cut into our action. Have you bumped into her on your travels?'

'Not yet.'

'She's trying to find our poteen still, I suppose.'

'She'll never find it. My little island is well off the beaten track.'

'If anyone can ferret it out, it'll be her.'

'Speaking of ferrets, how's the old man?' Willie smiled. 'I haven't seen him in a while.'

'Contrary as ever—whatever you do, don't give him any booze.'

'Chance would be a fine thing.'

Marcus began lifting the bags of potatoes into the boat. When the wooden baskets were empty, he turned Shergar around and headed back to the farm to fetch another load.

This had become a twice-monthly routine for the partners. Every second Monday, Willie would moor his yacht near the Nees' farm and pick up the potatoes. When the boat was loaded, Willie would raise anchor and head off to his home at the lighthouse on Rock Island, off the northwest coast of Inis Mór. They would meet up every Wednesday to bottle the poteen in the shed next to Willie's lighthouse and load the bottles onto the boat.

All they had to do was stay friendly with Garda Sergeant Gilligan, a functioning alcoholic who relied on their services as much as anyone. Marcus plied him with poteen every week in exchange for a general amnesty.

This weekly supply of booze to Gilligan also took care of Willie's accommodations at the lighthouse on Rock Island, a protected bird sanctuary that was out of bounds. Nobody bothered him because the island was cut off from Inis Mór on its north western tip and shielded from view by Brannock Island, which was located between the two. Whenever ornithologists turned up to study the local cuckoos, swallows or house martins, Willie would disrobe and dance around naked like a deranged hippy—that was enough to rid him not only of the ornithologists but also the birds.

Marcus liked the bootlegging routine and he enjoyed being entertained by Willie at his lighthouse. The old white tower had been abandoned for years but Willie had made the effort to return it to its former glory. It was full of books, *objets d'art* and oddities he had picked up during a lifetime of travelling the world. Marcus liked browsing through the library and he enjoyed the wonderful dishes Willie prepared when the work was done for the day. They would sometimes take Willie's boat to Kilmurvey or Kilronan and spend the night sampling the whiskies at Ivor's Pub before Marcus headed home through the fields.

It was the perfect set-up.

When Marcus and Shergar returned to the beach with another load of potatoes, Marcus held out the reins for Willie. 'Can you take it from here, your lordship? I'm late for Mass.'

Willie took the reins with a mischievous grin. 'Fair enough. Say a prayer for me.'

'I don't have that kind of time.' Marcus knew his old friend was a devout atheist and he suspected his soul was beyond redemption. They both laughed as Marcus looked off in the direction of Kilronan. 'What are you up to for the rest of the day?'

'Not much,' Willie said. 'I'm off to Galway tonight to do a bit of business. I'll be back on Wednesday for the bottling.'

'Is there anything wrong?'

'Nothing to worry about, old chap. I just have a few loose ends to tie up.'

Marcus waited for more information but all he could do was watch as Willie guided Shergar back up the hill towards the farm. He'd accepted that his friend was secretive and understood it was just a by-product of the poteen trade. It didn't do to have loose lips in the illegal alcohol business. If Willie had something to say, he would say it when he was ready.

It started raining when Marcus turned around and began his journey across the beach towards Kilronan.

TUESDAY

2

THE condensation made it almost impossible for Dykes to see through the windscreen. The glass just got foggier with every breath, no matter how long he wrestled with the car heater. He rubbed the windscreen to increase his visibility, but that afforded only a glimpse of the road ahead. There was no point rolling down the window because that would let in the rain and cold.

The rain had been falling on Galway city since dawn and the shining streets were clogged with rush-hour traffic. It was one of those miserable mornings when the only sane thing to do was defrost in front of the fire in a cosy pub.

Dykes needed a cigarette anyway, so he reluctantly rolled down the window and told himself the exercise would warm him up. Stamping his feet on the floor, he could still feel the cold through his thick socks and black brogues. He guided the navy-blue Ford Focus along Merchants Road, turning left onto Eyre Square. Traffic was getting heavier as he bullied the car through the one-way system. As he exited the square, he negotiated the bend onto Eglington Street, honking his horn at the oncoming cars. He was on his way to work, which was the last place he wanted to be.

Detective Sergeant Jim Dykes was a little too tall and too skinny for his own liking, with a gruff demeanour to which most people nevertheless took an instant liking. His wild, untidy hair had greyed in all the right places and his face had an understated elegance. He looked like a grumpy schoolmaster, a quality he often took advantage of when interviewing suspects. Dykes took pride in his appearance, but he was careful not to show it. Every six months, he purchased a new tweed suit off the rack at Anthony Ryan's Menswear and pretended not to care when people said he looked younger than he was.

His mood did not improve when a newsreader interrupted his favourite radio talk show with a hurried newsflash announcement. An unusual robbery had taken place at a nearby bank. Dykes kept his eyes on the road as he cranked up the volume.

'—*thieves got away with nearly two million euro in cash during a bizarre robbery this morning outside the Allied Irish Banks branch at Lynch's Castle in Shop Street. In a daring daylight raid, which bank officials were at a loss to explain, an unknown number of suspects walked away with two unattended bank sacks containing roughly one point eight million euro.*'

'Bloody hell.' Dykes could hardly believe his ears. *It can't be that easy to rob a bank in broad daylight*, he told himself. *I'm in the wrong line of work altogether.* He hoped Delaney would assign him the case so he could continue to ignore the piles of paperwork waiting on his desk. It would also make his final week on the job fly by in no time.

Dykes couldn't help but smile at the prospect as he guided the car along. One final case would give him an opportunity to make a triumphant exit from the force. He could hardly believe that a lifetime of police work and investigations would all be over in a matter of days. All he had to show for his illustrious thirty-five-year career as a police officer was a broken marriage and a gold medal he scarcely deserved.

He cursed when a woman came out of nowhere and crossed the street in front of him.

She reminded him of Anna—treacherous Anna—who had cheated on him throughout most of their fifteen-year marriage. Some detective he was—he hadn't cottoned on to the fact that his wife had been in love with another man—a pompous, penniless artist called Proinsias. He could have accepted the divorce if the reason had been more traditional: his job had been too much for her, perhaps; his drinking had gotten out of control, maybe; or his womanising had become embarrassing. He could have changed his ways. Adapted. But another man—he couldn't legislate against that.

To make matters worse, the ink on the divorce papers had barely dried when he'd been forced into retirement— something to do with budgets and paving the way for modern policing. And he didn't even have a house anymore. Anna got the lot—even the vintage MG and the cottage in Roundstone. But it hadn't been Anna's intention to leave him destitute—it was Proinsias who made sure the solicitors picked him clean.

Where was the justice in that?

When Anna had broken the news about her affair, Dykes had spent months trying to dig up some dirt on Proinsias. He had become so angry at the thought of this bearded freak sleeping with his wife that he resolved to do everything in his power to have him incarcerated. One night, he broke into the artist's studio and planted several ounces of cocaine in one of his paint boxes. Then he went to the pub and got blind drunk with the lads. By closing time, he was so overcome by guilt at what he had done that he broke back into the studio to retrieve the drugs. But he'd made so much noise and turned on so many lights that the neighbours called the Gardai. Dykes managed to hide the drugs inside his underpants by the time his colleagues arrived, but he still had to suffer the indignity of being caught in the act like a common criminal. If Anna had not forced Proinsias not to press charges, Dykes might have been thrown off the force and even imprisoned.

After that, he had been required to seek psychiatric help and was forced to accept the fact that he had lost Anna forever.

Dykes felt he didn't deserve to be treated like that by the woman he loved and the police force he cherished. He considered himself a model police officer: he gave his life to the Special Detective Unit; served the people and protected them when they were in danger; and was loyal to the officers under his command and respectful of his superiors. At least he could take some solace in the fact that Proinsias had no idea about the money Dykes had stashed away in his Post Office account—the money he would use to buy the boat that would help him ease his way into retirement.

Making his way up Mill Street, he spotted his new partner waiting in the rain.

Over the years, Dykes had come to view the whole concept of partners as counterproductive. Due to the unpredictable nature of police work, his superiors had always insisted detectives work in pairs, even though Dykes felt he worked better alone. This was Galway, he reasoned, not New York City or Johannesburg, where the police get shot all the time. The worst thing that could happen to him in Galway was that he might get a bad pint of Guinness. Not surprisingly, dozens of partners had come and gone during his career and he didn't like the look of the latest—and presumably the last—one.

Detective Sean O'Reilly had only been around for a few weeks and Dykes wasn't yet sure what to make of him. The detective accepted the fact that the age gap between himself and the new recruits was getting wider every year, but he couldn't understand why they had to be so enthusiastic and energetic. Dykes wasn't enthusiastic or energetic when he first joined the force—he was incompetent and thick in equal measure, and it took him years to fathom the job.

In Dykes's opinion, recently promoted detectives were overconfident and reckless, which weren't good traits to have when guns were involved. With his military haircut and designer clothes, O'Reilly was just the type to shoot first and ask questions later, Dykes thought. If experience was any guide, even more irritating traits would reveal themselves in short order.

'Morning, sir,' the younger detective said as Dykes pulled up outside Mill Street Garda Station. 'Superintendent Delaney told me to meet you here to tell you we're to head straight for the bank. Have you heard about the robbery?'

'Get in,' Dykes ordered. 'There's not a lot that goes on here I don't know about. We better get over there and see which one of those bastards is giving money away.'

O'Reilly did as he was told and threw his red duffel bag onto the backseat. He was jolted into his seat as Dykes accelerated and carried on along Dominick Street, nearly hitting an old lady in the process. Switching on the siren, the young officer braced for impact as Dykes shifted into high gear.

O'Reilly coward in his seat as Dykes went straight onto Bridge Street and made his way towards Shop Street. The young officer had only just passed his detective's exam and was excited about getting involved in a case so quickly. But he was also apprehensive, deciding he was better off standing back and letting his mentor call the shots.

He noticed a gold-coloured medal in the shape of a Celtic cross on the keyring attached to Dykes's car keys.

'Is that what I think it is?' O'Reilly asked, pointing to the medal.

'What do you think it is?

'The Scott Medal.'

Dykes nodded. In his late twenties, as a patrolman on the beat, Dykes had been awarded the prestigious medal, which honours acts of conspicuous bravery.

'Why do you keep it there?'

'I dunno—it makes a nice conversation piece.'

'How did you win it?'

'I'll tell you when I get to know you better.'

'What's the point in having a conversation piece if you don't want to have a conversation about it?'

Dykes frowned at his partner as he shifted into fourth gear.

The young officer tried to hide his trepidation as the Focus screeched to a halt outside Lynch's Castle, centimetres from the side of the building. The two officers got out of the car and waded through the throng of reporters.

The three uniformed Gardai on the scene knew enough to stay out of Dykes's way. They watched as the superior officer surveyed the scene and identified witnesses. O'Reilly followed his partner into the bank and kept pace with him every step of the way.

The first observation Dykes made about his new partner was that he had a round, chubby face and was more than a little overweight. For that reason, he didn't like standing too close to him in public because they looked too much like Laurel and Hardy. He hadn't heard it mentioned but he didn't like to invite the comparison. The young detective had also worn glasses, which Dykes considered inappropriate for police work. O'Reilly had been lucky the specific weight requirement to join the Gardai had been scrapped in favour of a physical competency test.

'By the way, sir.' O'Reilly held out his arm to hand Dykes a wad of cash. 'Here's the money you loaned me. I figured you'd need it if you have to put down a deposit on your new boat.'

'Good timing, lad' Dykes said, accepting the cash.

During their first week together as partners, O'Reilly had bored Dykes so much about the inadequacies of his new living quarters that the senior detective felt obliged to lend him the money to get his own apartment. O'Reilly described at length his flatmate's propensity for takeaway food, his inability to clean up after himself and his insatiable appetite for sex, usually with a different woman every night. Dykes felt he had no choice but to end the misery, both for himself and the young officer.

'Are you sure it won't leave you short?' Dykes said.

The young detective smiled and nodded his head. 'It's all sorted now. Have you seen the boat yet?'

'Not yet,' said Dykes, looking around to make sure no one was listening. 'I'm meeting the owner at the docks today.'

The uniformed officers stiffened as Dykes approached.

'What's the story, boys and girls?'

Garda Duignan, the oldest of the three uniforms, took out his black notebook and began to turn the pages.

'We think it was just one culprit, sir—some joker out for a morning stroll. Nobody saw anything. The Securicor yahoos are blaming the army boys and vice-versa. But if you ask me, they're equally to blame. Four of them were out there scratching their arses when the money was snatched and they all just lost their concentration at the same time.'

'Fair enough.' Dykes took another look around.

'Where's the manager's office?'

'Over there,' said Garda Barbara Casey. 'They're waiting for you inside.'

Dykes smiled at Barbara, who blushed as he leaned toward her.

'Are you on for a drink tonight?' Dykes whispered.

'Not tonight. I'm watching *Blue Bloods*.'

'Jesus. You can watch that any night.'

'I can go out with you any night, Jimmy. Tuesday is *Blue Bloods* night.'

Duignan smirked at Barbara as Dykes walked away, followed by O'Reilly. They stopped beside the coffee machine and Dykes put his hand on O'Reilly's shoulder. 'Mine's black with two sugars.'

O'Reilly frowned as Dykes carried on across the bank towards the manager's office. He organised the refreshments as Dykes opened the door and disappeared inside the office, closing the door behind him.

Duignan and the other uniforms watched as O'Reilly struggled with the coffee.

'How's detective work treating you, Sean?'

'It's better than standing around directing traffic all day.'

'Make sure you don't make a bollocks of that coffee or you'll be back on the streets.'

'Piss off, Duignan. Go and do some work, will you?'

Duignan and the other uniforms laughed as the young detective walked off with two mugs of coffee. They could barely contain their laughter as O'Reilly stopped in front of the manager's office and tried to open the door with his hands full.

'Oh, leave him alone,' said Barbara. 'He'll get there in the end.'

Finally, O'Reilly placed the coffee mugs on the floor and knocked on the manager's door. When there was no response, he opened the door. He glared at the laughing uniforms as he picked up the coffees and walked inside.

Dykes was in full swing when O'Reilly walked into the small office. O'Reilly hadn't been sure what to expect, as he'd never been in a bank manager's office before, but he was surprised to find it so compact and grey. Dykes barely had enough room to pace the floor as he admonished the three other men in the office.

Sitting behind the desk was Michael Roche, the bank manager. Occupying the other chairs were Colonel Oliver Prendergast, head of the First Infantry Battalion in Galway, and Brendan Casburn, head of Securicor's West of Ireland division.

'You mean to tell me some eejit was just out for a morning stroll and picked up two cash bags full of money?' Dykes barked at the three men. He turned around and grabbed a mug from O'Reilly.

'That's what I mean,' said Roche. The beads of sweat rolling down his face seemed to suggest he was buckling under the detective's interrogation. But it was clear he wasn't going to take all the blame. 'I had nothing to do with security.'

'It was the Securicor guards,' said Colonel Prendergast, who seemed to think attack was the best form of defence. 'They obviously just turned their backs for a second and the money was gone. My boys are not to blame here—their brief was to watch the street, not the money.'

The firearm attached to Colonel Prendergast's Defence Force-issue utility belt seemed to give his opinion more weight.

'Now hold on a second,' said Casburn, who wasn't carrying a firearm of any kind. 'My lads were in charge of transporting the money, not security on the ground. That was the Defence Force's job. They're the ones with the guns.'

Dykes was an experienced detective who thought he had seen it all. But for the life of him, he couldn't fathom the morning's events. His mind started to wander as he pictured the scene in his head. He could see the street, the bags of money and the pedestrian. But he couldn't make any sense of it.

'Tell me the rest,' Dykes barked at Roche.

'The Securicor agent jumped out of the truck, placed the sacks on the ground and waited for his colleague to accompany him into the bank.' Roche's head swivelled from side to side as he struggled to keep the pacing detective in his sights.

'Why did he put the sacks down?' Dykes was losing his temper. 'Why didn't he just hold on to the bloody things?'

'I think they were heavy, detective.'

'Why weren't the two soldiers on the scene watching the bags?' Dykes asked Colonel Prendergast.

'They were on the scene,' the colonel retorted, 'but they weren't supposed to be watching the fucking bags. They were supposed to be watching the street as the Securicor gobshites moved the bags. It must have been an inside job—that's the only explanation.'

When both Roche and Casburn started shouting in unison, Dykes grabbed a metal ashtray and slammed it down on the desk. 'Settle down, the pair of you,' he said.

Dykes didn't know what to make of it. There was no excuse for what had happened. The money was gone and nothing more could be done about it. The bank's insurers would insist on a full investigation, but the thief was unlikely to be caught. The serial numbers on the cash were consecutive but no thief would be foolish enough to start spending it without laundering it first. Dykes took another sip of his coffee and looked at the bank manager. 'I mean, is it even a crime? Technically?'

They all looked at Dykes but nobody knew what to say.

'Wasn't the money in the public domain when yer man picked it up?' Dykes said.

'I doubt the bank will see it like that,' said Roche.

'If you think of anything else, give me a shout.' Dykes opened the door and walking out of the office.

O'Reilly followed close behind as Dykes walked through the bank towards the entrance.

'Here's the tape from the security camera outside the bank,' said Duignan, handing it to Dykes.

The senior detective had a good look around as he walked through the ornately carved doorway and onto the street. He gestured to the assembled uniformed officers to move the onlookers back. Taking another sip of his coffee, he looked around and tried to visualise the crime. The sculpted Gothic gargoyles jutting out from the limestone building seemed to be mocking him as he tried to make sense of the situation. A hint of a smile crept across his face as he made eye contact with Barbara. She returned the smile and started to blush again.

Dykes noticed the CCTV cameras at either end of the street. They were too far away to be of much help, but he thought they would keep O'Reilly busy for a while.

'Get the footage from those two cameras, like a good man,' he told the young detective. 'We won't see much but you never know.'

He placed his coffee mug on a window ledge outside the bank and gestured for O'Reilly to do the same. 'Let's go.' Dykes got back into the car and turned on the ignition.

3

THE congregation listened as the Mass drew to a close. The priest struggled to make his voice heard above the loud dripping noises emanating from the various buckets spread across the floor. The old building was in a bad state of repair despite the priest's best efforts to rectify the situation.

'The Lord be with you,' the priest said, raising his arms.

'And also with you,' the congregation replied.

'May almighty God bless you, in the name of the Father, the Son and the Holy Spirit.'

'Amen.'

'The Mass is ended. Go in peace.' The priest turned to walk in front of the altar and, in the process, almost tripped over Judas, who had been lying in wait at the side of the altar for the duration of the Mass.

'Jesus Christ,' Father Marcus Nee muttered under his breath, much to the surprise of those members of the congregation who were close enough to hear. Judas scampered away and made his way down the aisle.

Marcus straightened himself, moved out from behind the pulpit and positioned himself at the edge of the altar. Everyone stood up and turned toward the centre aisle, ready for a quick getaway. Then Marcus raised his arms and lowered them with his palms facing downward to direct the congregation to remain seated.

'My friends,' Marcus said at the top of his voice, 'I was hoping you could hang on for a minute so we could have a little chat.'

The congregation sat back down again and waited for Marcus to get on with the lecture. They were used to his 'little chats' at the end of Mass, especially when they were joined by stray tourists who might have money to donate. Apart from the odd migrant newcomer, only a few people attended Mass on weekdays, especially since the heating oil had run out. And it was always the same people: Garda Sergeant Seamus Gilligan always sat towards the back of the church, far enough that the priest couldn't hear his erratic snoring. Every time he nodded off, his snoring would wake him up with a start. Then he'd nod off again and the cycle would continue for as long as he was stationary. Margaret Sheridan, the village postmistress and part-time church cleaner, always sat in front of Gilligan, and Mattie Dwyer, owner of the island's only bicycle rental shop, sat in front of her.

Father Tom O'Flaherty, Marcus's predecessor, always sat at the front on his own. Father Tom was well into his nineties and had retired as the parish priest several years earlier. Ever since Marcus returned from Rome to take over from Father Tom, he'd allowed the old man to stay at the parochial house, vowing to keep him there for as long as he was alive. This seemed like the most sensible solution to Marcus, who had to stay at the farm to keep an eye on his father.

'As you can see, we are still having trouble keeping the church in one piece,' Marcus explained.

The villagers shifted in their seats as they struggled to keep warm.

'We still need help,' said Marcus, who was running out of ideas to raise the money he needed to repair the Church of Saint Brigit and Saint Oliver Plunkett.

Try as he might, he couldn't squeeze any more money out of the archdiocese. But he was determined to use every trick in the book to realise his dream of bringing the church back to its former glory. He owed it to the islanders to save the beautiful bluestone church, which had been dedicated in 1905. When Saint Oliver was canonised in 1975, his name was added to Saint Brigit. The church was restored in 1978 and was long overdue a new roof.

The après-Mass lecture on the parish's lack of funds had become a regular occurrence at the church. Everyone on the island liked Marcus and thought he was one of the best priests they'd ever had, but it seemed to them that he was spending too much time trying to extract money from them. It wasn't as if they didn't care about the church; it was just that there was only so much they could do.

The place was falling down, right enough. But it would take a lot more money than these villagers possessed to fix it up.

As Marcus scanned his surroundings while delivering his speech, he was reminded of the magnitude of the disrepair. A disturbing proportion of the church floor was covered with buckets of varying size and colour. The walls and floor were also speckled with light as the sun shone through the holes in the roof.

'As I've told you before, neither the archdiocese of Tuam nor the bishop seem able to help us. This church is over a hundred years old, and we must preserve it.' Marcus tried to vary his tone, but he detected a general lack of interest among his flock.

'As you know, I have exhausted all possible resources to raise the money. You must make it known to your relatives and friends abroad that, unless they help, there might not be a church for them to return to. You must encourage them to give to the church renovation fund.'

Margaret and Mattie struggled to hide their irritation. They had been sitting in the damp church for over half an hour, and there was no end in sight.

'What does he expect us to do?' Mattie whispered. 'He's been banging on about the bloody roof for ages. Does he think we're made of money?' Margaret sniggered, knocking over her umbrella and waking Sergeant Gilligan, who leaned over to reprimand her.

'Shut up the pair of you. Can't you see I'm trying to pray?'

Margaret shrieked as she caught the foul smell of alcohol from Gilligan's breath. She spotted the small Virgin Mary-shaped holy-water bottle beside him. Grabbing the bottle, she opened the lid and smelled the contents. With a smirk on her face, she threw the bottle at Gilligan. 'I'm surprised you can string two words together with all that drink in you.'

'Jesus, it's fuckin' cold in here,' Mattie said as he rubbed his hands together.

Everyone turned towards Mattie, who realised he had spoken too loudly.

'We don't have enough money for oil, Mattie,' Marcus explained. 'That's why it's cold.'

Mattie buried his head in his hands in embarrassment.

'Did you have any luck getting money from your nephew in New York? The fancy Wall Street stockbroker.'

Mattie looked up, surprised that the priest was speaking to him.

'You may speak,' Marcus pushed.

'Cash flow problems, Father. He said the market would rebound in the next quarter after the Fed rate cut and the devaluation of the Chinese yuan.'

Marcus looked toward heaven. 'Well, we'll pray for that then.'

The priest waved his arm and began walking down the side of the church towards the front door.

'All right, you may go.' Marcus stopped at the confession box and grabbed a wicker basket filled with Virgin Mary-shaped holy-water bottles. Walking towards the back of the church, he passed through the large wooden door and waited on the church steps. Greeting the congregation as they filed out, he made sure to have a handshake and a quiet word for everyone.

The priest handed each of the faithful a holy-water bottle and accepted in return a five-euro note. He spotted Gilligan trying to sneak out behind Margaret.

'Ah Seamus, I'm glad I caught you.' He grabbed the garda sergeant by the arm and ushered him back into the church foyer.

Gilligan was a distinctive-looking fellow who found it difficult to go unnoticed in any surroundings. He had a mop of shocking red hair that glowed in the sunshine like a neon light. His oversized pot belly and short stature made him look like a human football and caused him to walk with a distinctive waddle.

'Lovely Mass, Father. You're a wonderful speaker altogether. I was on the edge of my seat.'

'Good man, Seamus. Listen, I'm still a bit worried about Lucy. Have you made any headway finding her?'

'Sorry about that, Father. I'm searching for her morning, noon and night. But I'm on my own abroad at the station with no one to help me but Fidelma.'

'I knew I could count on you.'

Marcus slapped Gilligan's hand when the police officer tried to extract one of the bottles from the basket.

'Sorry Seamus, you've had your quota now for today.'

'You're as sharp as a tack altogether, Father, I'll give you that.' Gilligan stumbled down the steps, almost tripping on the last one.

'Mind how you go there,' Marcus said.

'Don't worry, Father. I know what I'm doing.'

Marcus felt sorry for Gilligan and always had the feeling he was living in Inis Mór against his will. The sergeant had fallen out with his superiors in Galway years before and was doomed to spend the rest of his career on the island. To a Garda sergeant, he imagined, the Aran Islands was the same as Siberia to a Russian soldier.

Marcus had almost fully recovered from the 'Catholic' guilt he had endured in his efforts to keep his church intact. He worked hard in his poteen business, but that was only because he needed to make money for the church. He was saddened by the fact that most of his parishioners were heavy drinkers, but there was nothing he could do about that. They were going to buy poteen anyway, so they might as well be helping the church while they were at it.

He struggled with the underhanded nature of his tactic of distributing the poteen in holy-water bottles, but he considered it necessary for his customers to consume the illegal alcohol without drawing undue attention. He told himself he was protecting their reputations and providing them with spiritual comfort every time they gazed upon the image of the Virgin Mary.

He had also made his peace with the unethical lengths to which he had to go to ensure his poteen business flourished. He had become adept at controlling Sergeant Gilligan and making sure he kept the competition in line.

Marcus ensured that Gilligan was well supplied with poteen so he would not only allow his still to operate without hindrance but also shut down any rival operations that threatened to undercut his business.

He didn't feel so guilty about his other nefarious activities because they occurred well away from the grounds of the church. Marcus always consoled himself with the fact that all the money he earned went to buying materials to fix the church.

During his time at Trinity College and later at the seminary in Maynooth, Marcus had never imagined his priestly duties would have involved so much disreputable activity. He wondered what Father Antonio, his mentor at the Irish College in Rome, would have made of his undertakings. He would have forgiven the poteen distilling, but not the bribing of garda sergeants.

Marcus had spent only two years at the Irish College, but Father Antonio had become a trusted advisor and a major influence in his life. It had been Antonio who persuaded Marcus's tutors at Saint Patrick's College to let the young student continue his studies in Rome after only four years in Maynooth. The Italian was impressed with Marcus's grasp of theology and political science and with his gift for languages, especially Latin and Italian. He had always thought Marcus could best serve the priesthood in a political capacity in Vatican City.

Marcus had been an exceptional student, a fact first noticed by his schoolteachers in Aran. They had noticed he'd been leagues ahead of the other students, and they had arranged for him to attend a boarding school run by the Jesuits in Galway city. The 'Jes' had not only helped Marcus to hone his rowing skills, it had also helped him to clarify his vocation and smooth his path into the priesthood. From there, Marcus had studied theology and political science at Trinity before attending the seminary in Maynooth, where he'd met Father Antonio.

After only two years in Rome, though, the young priest had had to return home to Inis Mór when Eamon lost his leg. As it turned out, Father O'Flaherty was well past his retirement age by then, and the bishop was having trouble finding a replacement. So, Marcus's homecoming had been a godsend for all concerned. Marcus blamed neither his father nor Father Tom for stalling his career, but he still looked forward to the time when he could return to the pomp and political intrigue of life in the Eternal City.

Gilligan being the last parishioner out of the church, Marcus went back inside. He didn't bother closing the doors in case anyone wanted to go inside to pray or light a candle for a loved one. He had gotten into the habit of opening the doors of the church at seven o'clock every morning and leaving them open as late as possible every night.

Walking up the aisle to the sacristy, he rearranged several buckets as he went. He unlocked the door, opened it and walked inside.

The sacristy always had to be locked because it housed the priest's vestments, candles, sacrificial wine and various other ecclesiastical accoutrements. It was also used to store another commodity close to Marcus's heart.

He opened a large cupboard at the side of the room. On one side was an assortment of glass bottles filled with poteen, and on the other were thousands of Virgin Mary-shaped holy-water bottles, all stacked in even rows on the shelves. Marcus took off his Mass vestments and folded them. He placed them in the wardrobe and grabbed a chair from under the table. Placing the chair in front of the cupboard, he sat down.

Taking out a poteen bottle, he placed it on the floor beside him, then he grabbed a handful of plastic holy-water bottles and put them on the floor beside the bottle. Opening the poteen bottle, he took out a small funnel from the bottom of the cupboard. He unscrewed the lids of several of the holy-water bottles and then, using the funnel, proceeded to pour the poteen into the plastic bottles.

He repeated the procedure a few dozen times until the floor was covered with plastic Virgin Mary bottles full of poteen.

Marcus was startled when the sacristy door swung open and in limped Father O'Flaherty.

'You frightened the life out of me, Tom,' Marcus stood up to greet the visitor.

'That was a lovely Mass, Marcus.' O'Flaherty sat down on the chair Marcus had just vacated. 'A lovely Mass altogether.'

Marcus reflected on the fact that, in Irish society, potatoes and the sacrament of Mass were similar in that no matter what condition they were in or how they were presented, people always commented on how lovely they were. Marcus wondered if the old priest even noticed that the floor of the church was covered in plastic buckets.

'You don't mind if I take a few of these holy-water bottles, do you?'

Marcus panicked for a second and realised he had to think on his feet. 'Sorry Tom, those are all accounted for. I'll get you some water from the holy-water font at the front of the church.'

'But these are just sitting here,' O'Flaherty kneeled and grabbed a couple of the plastic bottles.

Marcus approached the old priest and relieved him of the cache.

'Let's go out to the church, Tom, and I'll get you some holy water from the font.' He helped the old man to his feet and guided him out the door.

'Where's your walking stick?'

'Ah now, thereby hangs a tale. I was—' O'Flaherty's voice tapered off as they walked through the church.

4

THE detectives' squad room at Mill Street Garda Station was quiet as Sergeant Dykes sat at his desk reading the *Connacht Tribune*. He was leaning back on his chair with his feet perched on the desk. His partner, O'Reilly, was sitting at the adjacent desk, trying to look busy.

The contrast between the two desks could not have been more striking. O'Reilly's space was neat and tidy, with everything in its proper place, while Dykes's area was messy and disorganised, with papers and food containers strewn across every available space.

'Did you check all of them?' Dykes asked.

'Yes, sir. The footage from the camera outside Powell's Four Corners was too blurry to make out and the one outside Lazlo's was broken.'

'That's alright. I think I got all I needed from the cameras at the bank.'

Having reviewed several tapes from the bank, Dykes felt he was in full possession of the facts. He was able to better explain how a man out for a morning stroll was able to pick up two cash bags full of money under the watchful eyes of four armed men.

The senior detective reflected on the unusual events of the day. He and O'Reilly had spent most of it interrogating witnesses. They questioned the bank's customers, the employees and the Defence Forces personnel, and they even had a lengthy conversation with the Securicor agents. But nobody had seen anything.

The newspaper rustled as Dykes turned the page. He groaned at the lead story on page three. It was dominated by an unflattering picture of Dykes standing outside the bank and a headline that barked *Daylight Bank Snatch Baffles Gardai*. Two of his colleagues, detectives McDonagh and McGuinness, had a snigger at his expense. Dykes noticed they had already taken the liberty of drawing a moustache on Dykes' picture.

'I think it suits you,' said McDonagh.

'What does 'baffles' mean, Jim?' asked McGuinness, peering out from behind his own copy of the newspaper.

Now that he knew how the crime was perpetrated, Dykes dismissed the robbery as another bizarre twist in the saga of the city. He predicted it would not be solved, and felt the bank deserved to be robbed for hiring such careless simpletons. One thing was sure, he thought, it wasn't a job for Special Branch. Dykes cast his mind back to his heyday on the force and wondered how, in less than a decade, he had gone from serving in the close protection detail of the president of Ireland to investigating bogus bank heists.

He was just about to reply to his colleagues' barbed comments when his phone rang.

'Yes sir,' he said, standing.

He put down the phone and smirked at his colleagues as he collected various items from his desk. 'You're just jealous because you're not as photogenic as me.'

He gathered up his notes and walked across the office, knocking on the superintendent's door before walking in.

Superintendent Frank Delaney stopped what he was doing and stared at Dykes.

Dykes was just about to sit down when Delaney raised his hand.

'You won't be here that long. Just tell me what you found on the security tapes.'

Dykes steadied himself and prepared for the big reveal.

'The person responsible for this whole mess was a bank clerk by the name of Dervla O'Leary.'

Delaney waited for more.

'Dervla arrived for work yesterday at eight forty-six in the morning, which is the same time as the bags were snatched.'

'So, she's our thief?' asked Delaney.

'No sir. When she arrived at the bank wearing...' Dykes checked his notes, '... a black Vera Wang strapless evening gown and Jimmy Choo high-heeled shoes, the four men who were supposed to be watching the money were watching her. It was at that precise moment that our suspect passed by and grabbed the money.'

'It couldn't have been that easy.'

'I interviewed her at length and felt comfortable removing her from our inquiries. She was at a function at the Radisson Hotel the previous night and went to work in the same clothes with the intention of changing when she got to the bank. I don't think she slept at her own place last night, if you know what I mean.'

Delaney thought about it for a moment. 'Let's just stick to the facts. Do you have anymore?'

'No, sir. The two Defence Forces privates have been court-martialled, the Securicor boys have been fired and the lovely Dervla has been suspended from work pending an internal inquiry.'

Dykes thought he knew his boss as well as anyone, but he didn't know how to gauge the superintendent's mood at that precise moment in time.

'It wasn't a robbery per se,' Dykes said. 'I mean, yer man just picked up the money and walked away with it. He didn't go into the bank and steal it, did he?'

'That doesn't matter,' Delaney barked. 'This clown has made a fool of us. I want him found and I want it all sorted,' the superintendent's face was red with rage, 'by the end of the week.'

It didn't sit well with Dykes that nobody—not even his own men—could explain how the suspect managed to walk away with one point eight million euro in broad daylight. But there was a limit to what he could do.

The day had taken its toll on him. The headache that had been threatening hit with the force of a sledgehammer. He stood bolt upright in Delaney's office as his superior launched into a lengthy monologue about the reputation of the Specialist Crime Directorate and the Gardai, and how important it was that they solve the case.

O'Reilly sat patiently at his desk waiting for his partner to reappear. While he was still learning his way around his new job, he was confident he was in the right place to gain the experience he needed. He was a thoughtful young man with a university education, which made him unsuitable for his current line of work. Despite his lack of experience, he was confident his brain would make up for what he lacked in physical prowess.

The young detective rose from his chair when Garda Barbara Casey suddenly appeared in front of him. 'How are you getting on with Dykes?'

'Fine,' said O'Reilly. 'Thank you. Yes, fine.'

Much to his surprise, he had developed a crush on Garda Casey in the short time he had been stationed in Galway. She was always the centre of attention when she walked into a room and she spoke with a Dublin accent that could peel paint off a wall.

'You can learn a lot from him, you know.'

'Is that so?' O'Reilly smiled. 'I'm already learning how to drive like a lunatic.'

'You should wipe that bleedin' smile off your face and pay attention.'

O'Reilly did as he was told and sat back down in his chair to regain his composure.

'I want you to do me a favour.'

'Sure. Anything.'

'This is Jim's last week. He's had a rough few months, so I don't want you giving him any trouble. Help him out. At least, don't make things any harder for him.'

O'Reilly studied Barbara for a moment. It was no secret that she and Dykes were an item, but he couldn't figure out what she saw in him. *She's beautiful and Dykes is definitely not in her league. Why does she care about a worn-out old copper like him?*

Without thinking, O'Reilly said the first thing that came into his head. 'Would you go out with me sometime?'

'I would in me arse,' she said.

The look of horror on her face surprised even O'Reilly. 'Why not?'

'What are ye like? You're only a feckin' chisseler…wet behind the ears.'

Barbara moved a few steps away from O'Reilly when Dykes returned from Delaney's office.

The superintendent's words were still ringing in Dykes's ears when he returned to his desk; nevertheless, his day began to look a little brighter when he saw Barbara waiting for him.

'Did you go and see that yacht of yours yet?' Barbara whispered in his ear.

Dykes smiled and looked up at her. No matter how angry he was, he always had time for Barbara. Nobody fit into a garda uniform quite like her, even when equipped with the full arsenal of extendable baton, pepper spray and handcuffs. He's lost count of the number of times he'd dreamed about being 'apprehended' with those handcuffs.

'Yes, I did,' Dykes smiled. 'I put down a deposit this evening, in fact.'

'You're a lucky man. You're getting out before you're too old to enjoy your retirement.'

'It's not as if I had a choice,' he said. 'I lost my wife, my job and my house, all in the space of a few months. But at least I have you.'

'And you'll always have me.'

Dykes recalled the good times they'd had over the years. Of all the people he knew in Galway, she was the only one he would miss. Whenever they went to the pub after work, Barbara was always up for a laugh. If he had ever intended cheating on his wife, Barbara would have been the one. But he was careful not to lead her on or allow her to get too dependent on him. Barbara helped him through his divorce, and he would always be grateful for that.

'Not today, alas,' he said as the phone rang. He answered the call and scribbled the details down on his notepad.

'Yeah, yeah,' he looked at his watch. 'Yeah, okay. Thanks.' He put down the phone, smiled at Barbara and turned to O'Reilly.

'Come on, we're going on a trip. Our man used a five-hundred-euro note from the robbery to pay for lunch this afternoon at Neo along the docks. The pub just lodged its evening takings, and the serial numbers rang the alarm bells.'

Dykes looked over towards the corner of the station and spotted a young man with long hair wearing a black Sawdoctors T-shirt. 'Gerry Brady!' he shouted. 'Come hither!'

Brady did as he was told and approached Dykes.

'You're coming with us—we're going to need a sketch artist.'

'Fair enough.'

The three men made their way across the office to the lifts. Dykes had to admit this new lead added a spring to his step. He knew he would miss the thrill of the hunt, but he had no intention of begging for his job back. He would just have to get used to retirement and his new life on the new boat.

5

WHEN the blue Ford Focus pulled up outside Neo, Dykes got out and waited for O'Reilly to follow him. He watched as his partner reached for his red duffel bag in the back of the car.

'I don't know why you have to bring that bloody bag everywhere with you,' Dykes asked as O'Reilly got out of the car and closed the door.

'Where else can I keep my handcuffs, gun and sandwiches? I'll never get used to carrying that bloody shoulder holster.'

Dykes checked his own shoulder holster to make sure his gun was in place as both men entered the pub.

'Do I need a gun?' Gerry Brady gathered his sketchpad and pencils and followed the detectives inside.

Dykes was glad of the warmth when the three men entered the dimly lit restaurant and sat a table by the huge window. The window took up nearly the entire wall, affording diners a panoramic view of the docks and the massive container ships that came from all over the world.

Neo was a spacious restaurant with well-appointed dining tables that seemed to cater to discreet couples.

Dykes took out his warrant card when the waiter approached. 'We're here about a five-hundred euro note that passed through this bar this afternoon. What's your name?'

'Just call me Truck. I remember the hundred euro—we only had one of those today. We had a job trying to change it.'

'Can we order some Cokes?' Brady asked. 'I'm dying with the thirst.'

Dykes shot Brady a furious look. 'What time was that?'

Truck scratched his head and looked around the bar. 'You'll have to ask Delores. She was in charge of the lunches this afternoon. Hang on a minute.'

Dykes, O'Reilly and Brady waited as Truck went off to get Delores.

'What would you do with one point eight million euro?' O'Reilly asked his partner.

'Don't be stupid. Where would I get that kind of money?'

'I was just thinking,' said O'Reilly, 'that prick is walking around town now wondering what to do with all that money. I bet he has no idea we're on his trail.'

'What would *you* do with the money?' Dykes asked.

'Of course, I'd have a hard time spending it without alerting the authorities. I wouldn't spend the money for a long time—not till the dust settled. I'd put it in one of those private Swiss bank accounts.'

'Do people still open Swiss bank accounts?' Brady asked. 'I thought that was only in the movies.'

'"Course they do,' said O'Reilly. 'Where do you think those bastards in the government keep all their brown envelopes?'

Dykes looked out the large window and admired the container ships moored at the docks. He considered his partner's question. 'You couldn't do much with one point eight million. Not after the banks, the solicitors, the taxman and the relatives got their cut. If I were as rich as Bill Gates or that guy who invented Facebook, then I could start having some fun.'

Too afraid to do anything else, O'Reilly and Brady listened intently.

'I'd buy one of those out-of-commission aircraft carriers from the U.S. Navy and a couple of old fighter planes. I could go anywhere I wanted and nobody would be able to shift me. I could moor the boat off the coast of Dublin if I wanted and helicopter into the city for my groceries.'

Dykes allowed himself to imagine what his life would be like in retirement. There would be worse places than the south of France, sitting on the deck of his new yacht, soaking up the sun and enjoying a glass of wine. He could embark on the occasional sojourn to the mainland to visit the casinos or the wine shops.

His retirement plan only started to take shape when he saw the yacht advertised in the paper the previous week. She would be moored at the Galway docks for one day only, the owner had said, and Dykes had gone to have a look without intending to commit. But he hadn't been disappointed with what he'd seen. When he'd clapped eyes on the vessel, he'd immediately fallen in love with her. Determined to have her, he'd put down a deposit straight away. Now he was determined to sail across Galway Bay and say goodbye to his ex-wife, to Ireland and to all the criminals with whom he had tangled for most of his life.

In his local pub, he had tried to regale his friends with stories of his imagined new James Bond lifestyle. He'd even gone as far as ordering a dry Martini, but the lads had given him such a hard time he reverted to his usual Guinness. He wouldn't have much money left over after buying the yacht, but he would be able to rely on his pension from the Gardai.

'I think I would—' Brady was interrupted mid-sentence when Dykes gave him a dig in the ribs to alert him of Truck's return.

The three men stood when Truck returned with Delores.

'This is Delores,' Truck said, pulling up an extra chair.

Delores sat down and gestured for the others to do the same. 'Do you want anything to eat?'

A hefty woman with a remarkable bosom, Delores looked like she was in her mid-fifties despite the liberal amount of makeup she was wearing. Her clothes were loose-fitting and dark, as if she were trying to hide her ample girth. She spoke with a thick Kerry accent that seemed to put Dykes more at ease. *If you can't trust a Kerry woman*, he thought, *who can you trust?*

Dykes nodded his head. 'We won't keep you long.'

O'Reilly grabbed a breadstick from the table as Dykes took out his notebook.

'Can you describe the man who passed the five-hundred-euro note?'

Dykes looked shocked when Delores started sniggering. He shifted in his seat and glared at the woman. 'Did I say something funny?'

'It's just that you make it sound like he produced it out of his arse.' Delores wiped a tear from her eye and smudged her mascara in the process.

'Answer the question, please.'

'I didn't really get a good look at him. The place was dark, and he was wearing a baseball cap that hid his face. He looked like he was fairly old.'

'What type of baseball cap was he wearing?

'It was blue…with something written on it. I think it was *Fart* or *Fort* or something like that.'

'Or *Ford*, maybe,' said O'Reilly.

'That was it,' said Delores, unable to hide her embarrassment.

'Can you remember what time the man was here?' Dykes asked.

Delores reached out her hand and placed a receipt on the table. 'I don't have to.'

Dykes looked at the receipt and saw it was issued at two thirty-two in the afternoon. 'And you're sure this was our man?'

'Yes, we don't get many five-hundred-euro notes.'

'I'll have to keep this for our records. Do you mind helping our sketch artist with the description?'

Delores shrugged her shoulders and watched as the two detectives rose from their seats.

'Can you make your own way back to the station?' Dykes asked Brady.

The sketch artist nodded his head and reached for his pencils.

'Thanks for your help, Delores. If you think of anything else, just give me a call.' Dykes handed her his business card, and the two detectives made their way out of the pub.

Dykes lit up a cigarette when they were out in the open air.

'Which one is yours,' O'Reilly asked as he looked out across the docks.

'She was moored over there all day and now she's gone. The owner must have just left.'

Dykes handed his partner the car keys and watched as O'Reilly opened the door and climbed in the passenger side. The detective took another drag and followed the smoke with his eyes as it rose into the air and disappeared into the moonlight.

II

At that same moment on the Aran Islands, Eamon Nee was also watching the moon. He was jolted from his thoughts by a loud banging sound that seemed to emanate from the church. He watched as the old priest exited the main door of the church and eased his way to the steps. Eamon could feel the chilly night air in his old bones as he struggled to keep warm. From his vantage point inside the gate of the parochial house, he waited as O'Flaherty negotiated the steps and crossed the road. He opened the gate as the old priest approached and allowed him to enter.

'Did you get the holy water?'

'I did,' said O'Flaherty, reaching into his pockets.

Eamon grabbed the bottles as soon as O'Flaherty presented them.

'I did what you asked. Now, where's my walking stick?'

Eamon reached into the bushes and grabbed the old man's walking stick.

'Sorry about that. I had to make sure you were properly motivated.'

O'Flaherty took back the walking stick as Eamon opened the lid of one of the holy-water bottles. He put the bottle to his mouth and drank the contents. As soon as he tasted it, he spat it out.

'What the hell is this?' Eamon opened the other bottle and had the same reaction.

'It's holy water. What did you expect?'

In a fit of rage, Eamon balanced himself on his good leg and tried to grab O'Flaherty's walking stick. But the old priest was too quick for him; he managed to raise the stick and hit Eamon over the head with it. Eamon fell to the ground and scattered the holy-water bottles across the path.

'What the hell are you playing at, you geriatric fool? Why couldn't you just go over and get your own holy water?'

'Marcus won't let me have anymore.'

'What do you mean?' O'Flaherty lowered his arms to allow Eamon to grab on and pull himself off the ground. 'There's plenty of it in the church font and the sacristy is full of bottles.'

'Where did you get this stuff?' Eamon grabbed onto the gate and dusted himself off.

'From the church font, of course.'

'I don't suppose you'd go in again and get me some of the bottles from the sacristy.'

'Marcus says they're accounted for. He won't let me have them.'

'Can we wait until he leaves and then sneak in?'

'Marcus has the only key to the sacristy. What's so special about those bottles?'

Eamon stared at O'Flaherty and decided discretion was the better part of valour.

'Ah well, you see, the water in those bottles is blessed by the bishop,' Eamon smiled at his own inventiveness, 'and the water in the font is blessed by Marcus.'

'What feckin' difference does that make? Marcus is a priest, isn't he?'

'Marcus is my son. It's a mortal sin to drink holy water blessed by your own blood.'

'I never heard of that before.'

'How do you think I lost my leg?'

'You must think I came down in the last shower.'

O'Flaherty considered the matter for a moment. 'How did you know this water was blessed by Marcus just by tasting it?'

'You can always tell when it's blessed by a relative. It tastes a bit like vinegar.'

'My Uncle Jarlath was a priest and his water never tasted any different.'

'Next time you're in the sacristy on your own, will you grab a few bottles for me?' Eamon opened the gate. 'Do you have any money?'

'I might have.'

'Let's go down to the pub. You can make it up to me by buying me a drink.'

Eamon opened the gate wider, and the two men limped off to the pub together.

WEDNESDAY

6

WILLIE sat on the flat limestone ground with his knees folded, allowing the wind to caress his naked body. With his eyes closed, he could hear nothing but the sound of the waves tumbling into the rocks below. Like a contented Buddha, he settled himself just a stone's throw away from the edge of an eighty-metre cliff.

He reached for his glass bong and placed the chamber over his mouth. Placing a finger on the hole at the side of the apparatus, he lit the weed with his brass Zippo. Sucking until the chamber was full of smoke, he took his finger off the side hole and continued to inhale.

He repeated the process several times, and then he lay down against the limestone. He marvelled at the wisps of white clouds as they paraded across the clear blue sky. The scene above was peaceful and calm until the vapour trail of a jumbo jet spoiled his view as it darted across the heavens on its way to America.

Rock Island had for years been a protected bird sanctuary, which meant nobody was allowed to live there or build dwellings.

Situated on the northwest tip of the Aran Islands, the outcrop was far enough away from Inis Mór to prevent anyone seeing what was going on there. Willie could be testing nuclear weapons on the outcrop and no one would ever know. The island was almost completely formed of limestone and had the occasional clump of grass here and there. The eastern side was accessible by boat, but the west was protected by sheer cliffs that loomed above sharp rocks and crashing waves.

Unfortunately for the birds, Willie had taken a liking to the place and had decided to make his home there. He had moved into the abandoned lighthouse on the west of the outcrop and had resurrected the pot-still in the shed at the back of the building.

Marcus and Gilligan were the only people who knew where Willie lived and, more importantly, where he worked. He wasn't doing any harm because he hadn't built any new structures, he told himself, he was only making use of what had already been there.

And the birds could take a running jump if they didn't like it.

Willie had once been a palaeontologist of note. He'd come down from Oxford sometime in the late Sixties and, instead of seeking gainful employment at the British Natural History Museum like he was supposed to, he'd ended up selling clothes to hippies on Carnaby Street.

After a brief stint in the British Army Catering Cops, where he spent the bulk of the time peeling potatoes, Willie managed to get his career back on track. He secured a grant from the museum and travelled to Inis Mór to search for the remains of prehistoric creatures he believed to be buried on its northern tip. But after years of digging, he'd been unable to further the cause of prehistoric discovery.

Instead, he found the hidden shed containing the old pot-still next to the lighthouse.

Since he'd run out of money and was unwilling to suffer the indignity of returning to London a failure, he had done what any eccentric old English palaeontologist would have done in his position—he'd cleaned up the pot-still and gone into business.

Willie had always considered himself unsuitable for most of the physical requirements of bootlegging. Ever since his days in the army, he hated peeling potatoes, and he had no time for horses—unless he could bet on them. That's where Marcus came in.

Now on the verge of seventy, Willie had the bulbous nose of a seasoned drinker and his eyes were often bloodshot. The top of his head was bald, but the sides had a healthy skirting of sandy hair that fell to his shoulders. Willie was not short of money, but that wasn't evident in the way he dressed.

The Englishman spent his days chugging along the coast, selling bottles of poteen to farmers and pub owners in hidden inlets. He seldom contemplated the illegalities of his endeavours; after all, he made a good living, and who would ever suspect an eccentric old English palaeontologist?

When the effects of the marijuana were beginning to wear off and he'd had enough of nature, Willie slipped on his brown corduroy pants and grabbed his tattered Aran sweater. He picked up the bong and the assorted paraphernalia and made his way back to the lighthouse.

He sniffed the fresh air as he went and admired the view of the ocean.

Willie liked to keep his yacht shipshape, with everything in its proper place, and the same could be said for the lighthouse. The spiral stone steps leading up to the living quarters were immaculate.

The *pièce de résistance* was the collection of framed manuscripts and illuminated maps hanging on the wall all the way up the spiral stairway. Each framed manuscript was hanging above its own light fixture, which brought out the splendour of the artwork.

To the casual observer, the manuscripts looked like genuine letters from historical figures that would no doubt fetch a pretty penny at auction. But Willie would never sell them at auction—because they were forgeries.

Willie had penned the manuscripts himself during his days in Carnaby Street. Being a dab hand at calligraphy and the techniques of the ancient scribes, he often made extra money selling 'historical documents' to hapless punters. He went to great pains to use only genuine materials that scribes in the sixteenth century would have used. He made his own sheets of parchment out of animal hide and quill feather pens that would fool even the most doubting art appraisers.

He once sold a duchess a love letter purported to have been written by Queen Elizabeth I to Sir Walter Raleigh. Even though Willie had only finished it the previous afternoon, the duchess paid two hundred pounds for it and said she would present it to Queen Elizabeth II at a forthcoming garden party. He always said his biggest claim to fame was that one of his masterpieces was hanging somewhere in Buckingham Palace.

Retrieving his shoes from the upstairs living room, he looked out the window and saw that Marcus had arrived. He ran downstairs to the poteen still so as not to keep his guest waiting.

The sea was as calm as a millpond as Marcus rowed his *currach* along the coast towards Rock Island. He eased the oars back and forth with poise and precision as the old craft glided on top of the water. He admired the sunset to the west and marvelled at the colours of Connemara to the east as the setting sun cast its final spell of the day.

It was getting dark when Marcus moored his *currach* at the makeshift jetty and tied her up alongside Willie's yacht. Climbing out of the boat and onto the yacht, he had a quick look below deck to make sure Willie hadn't left any bags of potatoes behind, and then he made his way to the stern. He jumped onto the jetty and began whistling a tune, the name of which he had long forgotten.

Walking up the hill towards the lighthouse, Marcus passed a sign that said: 'No Trespassing.' His dishevelled hair was blowing in the wind, and he wore an old black leather jacket to shield him from the cold. Willie had often observed that Marcus looked more like a windswept playboy than a priest.

'Anyone here?' Marcus opened the door to the shed and walked in.

'Over here, dear boy,' came the cry from behind the clanking metal still in the middle of the shed. 'How was your flock today?' Willie was loading the smashed potatoes into a large container connected to the still.

'There's nothing wrong with them that a few Hail Marys couldn't fix.'

Marcus grabbed a chair from the corner of the shed and sat down beside the still.

'I think my *currach* is on its last legs,' he said, unable to hide his disappointment. 'I've been concentrating so much on the church that I've been neglecting the bloody boat.'

'We all have our crosses to bear.' Willie immediately regretted what he'd said and rushed to qualify the offensive comment. 'Sorry, Marcus. Once an atheist, always an atheist.'

Marcus took off his jacket and rolled up his sleeves. He grabbed a handful of cut potatoes and dumped them into a large container of boiling water.

'That *currach* helped me win two All-Ireland titles. God knows it deserves to be looked after better than that.'

'Saint Peter was a fisherman, was he not?'

Marcus considered that for a second. 'What's that got to do with anything?'

'Well, I'm sure God wouldn't mind if you used some of the church's coffers to buy a new *currach*—as long as you used it for fishing.'

'I don't want a new *currach*. The point is, I wish I took better care of the one I have.'

Marcus grabbed another handful of potatoes and repeated the process.

'Is the first batch ready for tasting?'

'We are waiting only for your ecclesiastical direction.' Willie lifted a large jug from under the still and poured the clear liquid into two glasses, one of which he handed to Marcus.

They drank, and their eyes glazed over as they stared into the distance.

'You know what? I think we've cracked it!' And down went yet another mouthful.

'That's powerful stuff, Willie. I'd rather spend my time giving people spiritual guidance than getting them drunk on spirits, but that's powerful stuff.'

'The finest poteen in Ireland,' Willie said, pouring out two more glasses.

'Do they have poteen in England?'

'They have many varieties of homemade concoctions that go by many different names. The monks have been getting people drunk since before the Dark Ages.'

Willie emptied his glass and poured another round.

'You've never been to England, have you?' he asked.

'There are only two reasons why an Irish person would go to England: to have an abortion or to get a job. 'There are only two reasons why an Irish person would go to England: to have an abortion or to get a job. And I require neither.' Marcus smirked as he gulped down another mouthful.

7

IT WOULD be safe to say that Ivor's Pub was in the middle of nowhere. For the locals, it was more like a home than a pub. It was a one-room cottage with a small bar at one end, a large fireplace at the other, and rickety old tables and chairs in the middle. On the outside of the pub, there were no lights or any of the markings usually associated with licensed premises. It was situated on a remote stretch of road between Kilronan and Onaght, near the village of Kilmurvey. The isolation suited the island's late-night drinkers because Ivor's was so far out of the way that neither their wives nor their girlfriends could be bothered to travel to it.

Ivor's was known far and wide as an illegal after-hours venue. It was in no danger of being shut down because it fell under Marcus's umbrella of amnesty provided by Sergeant Gilligan, who himself was a regular customer.

Almost every day, two old donkeys could be seen grazing outside the pub. Whenever one of the locals got too drunk to walk home or ride his bicycle, he could climb on one of the donkeys and guide it home. Afterwards, the donkey would make its own way back to Ivor's and wait for the next drunken passenger.

As it was dole day, the bar was crowded with locals when Marcus walked in. He spotted Sarah Shannon straight away, but he wasn't ready to talk to her. She was sitting at a corner table with her back to him, so he decided to seek some liquid courage. Sarah was an old friend who had called him earlier to say she'd had something important to talk to him about. Since she didn't live on the island anymore, he wondered what could have been so important that she'd had to make a special trip to see him.

He saw his father sitting at the bar and made his way over. A heated discussion was raging nearby between two of the lads. Mattie Dwyer broke free from the row and stood in Marcus's path.

'Howya, Father?' Mattie struggled to stay on his feet. 'We were wondering if we could prevail upon your superior knowledge to settle a small dispute.'

Mattie was a stocky man who had the red, chubby cheeks of a regular drinker. He seemed to be always smiling, which made his cheeks even chubbier and more luminous. He often made the effort to dress well, but then he'd spoil the effect by wearing his tatty wellington boots with the tops turned down, even when he went to Mass. What made Mattie stand out, though, was his ill-fitting toupee. Marcus always found men who wore toupees difficult to take seriously. In the first instance, they were vain. And vanity is an unforgivable affliction in a man. Secondly, how could you have any respect for someone who thought nobody would notice it was a toupee?

'Certainly, Mattie. What is it?'

'Well, I was saying they should put more sex on the telly after nine o'clock. And McNamara here thinks I'm talking through my arse. What do you think?'

'I think you're both right.'

Dwyer stood upright in stunned silence as Marcus resumed his walk through the pub. His companion, McNamara, laughed and raised a glass to Marcus as he passed.

'Ah, what does he know?' said Dwyer. 'He wouldn't know a woman if she slapped him in the face.' They both laughed as Marcus rolled his eyes to Heaven.

Marcus found a stool beside his father and sat down.

'A pint please, Ivor, when you're ready, and one for the old man.'

'You're an hour late, by the way,' said Eamon.

'Sorry about that. The distilling took ages tonight— Willie seems preoccupied.'

Marcus leaned on the bar and studied his Guinness as it settled in the glass in front of him.

'This gobshite wouldn't serve me until you came in,' Eamon pointed at Ivor.

'I was under strict instructions, as you well know,' said Ivor, handing Eamon his hot whiskey.

Marcus watched as Ivor finished the job and placed the pint on the counter.

'Don't mind him,' Marcus said, handing Ivor five euros. 'His bark is worse than his bite.'

Ivor was a short, fat Canadian who seemed to always be sweating. Everyone liked him, even though he was a short, fat Canadian who seemed to always be sweating. He had travelled the world several times before settling on Aran to marry a local woman. She had been left the house when her parents died, and Ivor helped her turn it into a pub.

Marcus liked going to the pub because he enjoyed catching up on the latest gossip about his parishioners. There was always an amiable atmosphere and a generous fire in the corner. He looked around and took stock of the clientele. It was always busy when the unemployed islanders picked up their dole money.

He looked again at Sarah Shannon, sitting all on her own. Once upon a time, she had been the love of his life. They had been childhood sweethearts and, if it hadn't been for several unforeseen events, they might have spent the rest of their lives together. He tried to think about something else, but for some reason, he couldn't concentrate on his pint.

Marcus and Sarah had been inseparable as children and seemed to retain their special bond over the years, even when Marcus joined the priesthood. They'd gone to national school together on Inis Mór, attended secondary school together on the mainland, and had even gone to the same university. When Marcus had taken up political science at Trinity College, Sarah was there studying medicine.

But then Sarah got pregnant, and the father of the child disappeared. She had returned to Inis Mór to have her baby and Marcus had gone on to Maynooth and then to Rome. Marcus had often wondered what would have happened if Sarah had been able to continue in medicine. He had returned to the island later as a priest and had done his best to help Sarah with her child, Lucy. But Lucy had turned out to be more of a handful than either of them could ever have imagined. Marcus now suspected that Lucy was the reason for Sarah's sudden appearance.

Marcus returned his attention to his newly poured pint and deemed it ready to drink. Grabbing his Guinness, he drank half of it in one satisfying gulp and licked the froth from his upper lip with his tongue. He looked around the bar again and decided he couldn't put it off any longer. Getting up off his stool, he walked over to Sarah's table and sat down opposite her.

'Hello there,' he said. 'Fancy meeting you here.'

'Hello yourself,' Sarah answered, trying to sound casual.

Marcus studied his old flame as he placed his Guinness on the table. She was still beautiful after all these years, he thought. Her blonde hair and fair complexion had always made her stand out on an island of weather-beaten fishing folk. Marcus marvelled at how she always remained upbeat, even after years at the mercy of an abusive husband and an ungrateful daughter.

'How are things in the big city?' Marcus asked.

'Keeping busy—and yourself?'

'Not bad—still trying to keep the church from falling down around our ears.'

Sarah took a cigarette out of the box and offered one to Marcus. He accepted and then allowed her to light it for him.

'You know why I'm here?'

'I have a fair idea.'

'I'm sorry about the cryptic phone call earlier. I had to warn you about Lucy and come over myself to try to deal with her.'

Marcus reached across the table to take her hand. He held it and smiled. 'It's great to see you, but there was no need for you come all the way here. I can handle Lucy.'

'What about the boyfriend, Jimmy? What are you going to do about him?' Sarah asked after a long silence.

'I've asked Gilligan to keep an eye on them. Nothing else I can do.'

'She's still mad at you. She's trying to get back at you by destroying your poteen business. She tried setting up a rival business, and now she just wants to destroy yours. I can't talk any sense into her.'

'Don't worry about Lucy,' Marcus said, wishing he could take his own advice. 'Just stay away from her.'

'I'm worried what she'll do to you. And to Willie.'

Marcus blamed himself for the ongoing misadventures of Sarah's wayward daughter. He had tried many times over the years to give her guidance and inspiration, but she always seemed to repel anyone who tried to help. Now she was in cahoots with Jimmy Roberts, a thug from the North of Ireland who was old enough to be her father, and her activities were affecting Marcus.

Marcus knew that Lucy was a lot smarter than most people gave her credit for. He also knew he would have to watch his back because nobody could hold a grudge like Lucy.

'I'm sorry her behaviour has taken such a toll on you,' he said.

'You know what she's like. I don't want you to get hurt.'

'Don't worry about me.' Marcus looked at his watch.

He rose from his chair and stood upright.

'I have to go. Can I see you tomorrow?'

Sarah nodded and allowed Marcus to kiss her on the cheek.

He returned to the bar and sat back down next to his father. Distracted by the mumbling sounds that seemed to be coming from his father, he was unable to focus on the fresh pint Ivor had placed before him.

'What are you saying to me now?' Marcus asked.

'Nothing.'

No sooner had Marcus returned his gaze to the pint than the mumbling started again.

'You've clearly got something to say. Your lips are moving, and words are coming out of your mouth."

'I'm trying to organise my thoughts,' Eamon explained.

'Well, can you do it without making such a racket?'

'I have to do it like this. There's so much going on in my head that my thoughts are hard to distinguish from my hallucinations. I've been without drink for that long I'm starting to imagine things.'

'Something tells me there's not that much going on in that head of yours to begin with,' Marcus took a sip of his pint. 'Get it off your chest before my pint goes sour.'

'What's she doing here?' Eamon inquired.

'None of your business.'

'I hope you know what you're doing, son.'

'Well, there's been no evidence of it so far.'

'The last time you got involved with that woman, she broke your heart. And now her nasty daughter is gunning for you. I told you that poteen business was going to get the better of you. And it's no good for Willie either. You can't expect a man of his age to circumnavigate Galway Bay every week.'

'He says he likes it. Anyway, I'm too busy to do it.'

Marcus finished his Guinness and paid for it.

'And another thing...' Eamon raised his voice as Marcus rose from his stool and walked over to the side door, 'I don't think the bishop would appreciate you doing all these illegal jobs when you're supposed to be concentrating on your ecumenical duties.'

'Keep your voice down, would you? I'm off out to engage in another of my illegal activities. I'll see you later tonight.'

Marcus nodded at Ivor, who walked out from behind the bar and opened a small door at the back of the pub.

'And I'm sure using Mary, the blessed virgin, as a poteen receptacle is a mortal sin.'

Marcus glared at his father and turned to follow Ivor out to the yard.

'Don't mind him, Marcus,' Ivor said as he closed the back door. 'He's just pissed off about the restrictions you implemented. I'll cut him off after the next one.'

'I'm not worried about him,' Marcus smiled. 'I'm worried about the poor donkey that has to take him home.'

8

O'REILLY unwrapped the Mighty Mac with some haste and couldn't wait to sink his teeth into the succulent burger. He hadn't eaten all day, and not even the disapproving looks Dykes was shooting across the table could quell his appetite.

His guilty conscience would allow him to eat at Supermac's only once a week, and he was determined to enjoy the experience. This was a Galway institution and ever since he was posted to the city, he'd always made the weekly pilgrimage come hail or shine. It had been hard enough to convince his partner to let him have half an hour in his favourite fast-food restaurant, and he wasn't going to let him spoil the occasion.

'Why don't you eat something, sir?'

'I wouldn't put that shit in my mouth.' Dykes took a sip of his coffee. 'I have my groceries in the car. I was going to make some spaghetti bolognaise when I got home.'

O'Reilly picked up his strawberry milkshake and sucked up the velvet liquid through the plastic straw. Then he used both hands to grab the Mighty Mac and raise it to his salivating mouth.

Just then, Dykes's phone rang. Instinctively, O'Reilly placed the sandwich back down on the table and tried to listen in on the conversation.

'Yea, this is Dykes.'

O'Reilly grabbed the sandwich again and this time managed to bite off a sizeable chunk. He savoured the taste as he chewed and then he swallowed, washing it down with another mouthful of the milkshake. As he drank, he wondered if it would be possible to make a milkshake at home that tasted just as good.

'Is that confirmed?' Dykes asked over the phone. 'It's a long way to go if it's not confirmed.'

O'Reilly cleaned his mouth with a napkin. He took a plastic fork from the tray and picked up a forkful of garlic chips. He watched as Dykes put down the mobile and scribbled in his notebook.

Dykes picked up the phone again and scrolled down the list of numbers until he found the one he wanted. O'Reilly picked up the sandwich again and continued listening.

'Are you free tonight?'

O'Reilly couldn't hear the other end of the conversation, but he hoped it had nothing to do with work. They had been working all day, and he was hoping to go home for the night. It sounded as if Dykes was asking someone out on a date.

'I'll make you a nice dinner.'

Yes, it's definitely a date, O'Reilly thought.

'You owe me a favour, you bastard. If you let me down, I'll have to relocate all that evidence I misplaced and reopen your case.'

Maybe it's not a date after all.

Dykes rose from his seat and gestured for his partner to follow him outside. O'Reilly took another mouthful of garlic chips, followed by another bite of the Mighty Mac, and then he ran after his partner.

The young detective climbed into the Focus, which was parked on a double yellow line in the middle of Eyre Square. He watched as the senior detective paced up and down the street with the phone to his ear, stamping his feet on the ground to keep warm. Finally, Dykes put the phone back in his pocket and got into the car.

'You're not going to believe this.' Dykes put his key in the ignition. 'We're going to the Aran Islands.'

He reversed the car and drove down the street.

'Another five-hundred-euro note from the robbery turned up in a bar in Kilronan. The manager of the bar, a Mr Geraghty, lodged the money at his local bank. The serial numbers match.'

'So, we're going out to sea then?' O'Reilly asked. 'On a boat?'

'I'll tell you what; there are no flies on you.' Dykes drove the car around the square and down Victoria Street, turning right towards the docks.

'I know a man with a boat. He owes me a favour. You like boats, don't you?'

'Not really.' O'Reilly's face turned green at the thought of hurtling across the choppy sea in the middle of the night.

The tires screeched as Dykes guided the car around the corner and onto the docks. O'Reilly's stomach churned as they neared the edge of the docks and came to a halt next to an old trawler that looked like she was ready for the scrap heap. The young detective surveyed the old boat and then he noticed a grisly old fisherman standing on her bridge.

'You don't look so hot,' Dykes told O'Reilly as he switched off the car engine. 'You look about as good as that boat.'

'Please tell me we're not going out in that.'

O'Reilly laughed as he pointed at the old trawler to which his partner was referring. Then he stopped laughing when he saw the expression on Dykes's face.

The *Aran Angel* was the smallest and the oldest fishing trawler in the harbour that night. It had seen better days and looked as if it should have been scrapped years before. The paint, where there was paint, was peeling, and substantial portions of the deck were covered with the congealed remains of dead fish.

O'Reilly stared at it in disbelief and hoped Dykes was not considering crossing the sea aboard such an unsuitable vessel.

'Is it safe?'

'The skipper owes me a favour. It's the best we could do at short notice.'

'It could do with a wash,' O'Reilly said.

'Not a chance,' said Dykes. 'The dirt and the grime are the only things keeping this old bucket in one piece.'

Dykes gathered his bag of groceries and overnight bag, got out of the car and walked towards the *Aran Angel*. O'Reilly grabbed his red duffel bag from the back seat and stayed a step behind.

Chalkie White, the skipper, jumped off the boat and began untying one of the mooring ropes. Despite the cold night, he was dressed in a sleeveless sweatshirt that revealed muscular arms covered in illegible tattoos.

Chalkie looked about as haggard and dishevelled as the boat. He was tall and well built, but he carried himself like a man who had spent too many days in rough seas wrestling with tangled fishing nets and drunken deck hands.

'Just remember it wasn't my idea to cross the bay so late at night!' Chalkie shouted as the detectives approached. 'If we sink, don't come crying to me.'

'Good man, Chalkie,' said Dykes, shaking the skipper's hand. 'This is O'Reilly. Be gentle with him.'

Chalkie chuckled when he saw O'Reilly and the look of apprehension on his face. O'Reilly could just about make out the outline of a naked lady on the skipper's forearm.

'She's not the *Queen Mary*, but she's good enough for the likes of you.'

'Just as long as we don't run into any weather,' said Dykes. 'I don't think the lad could take it.'

The three men jumped onto the trawler, and all except O'Reilly hit the deck safely. The young detective landed on a piece of decayed fish and went skidding across the deck.

The detective was surprised to see a pair of manicured hands reaching down to pick him up, but they were too petite and too fragile to belong to Chalkie. When O'Reilly lifted his head and stared at the face that went with the hands, he was shocked to see a beautiful woman who looked to be in her early twenties.

'Ah, you met my daughter, Geraldine.' Chalkie picked up the shaken detective by the scruff of the neck and propped him up on the side of the boat. Geraldine flashed her father a disapproving look as he turned around the face Dykes.

'Dykesey, make yourself useful and help me get us underway,' said Chalkie. 'Ger, take him up to the wheelhouse out of the cold.'

But before they could go any further, O'Reilly vomited on Geraldine's boots. The young woman smiled, stepped over the mess and reached for a rag. 'It's going to be a long night.'

When they reached the wheelhouse, Geraldine guided O'Reilly onto the leather skipper's chair in front of the wheel. She made coffee and added whiskey to it before handing the mug to the young detective.

She took off her oilskin fisherman's jacket to reveal a silk negligée tucked inside a pair of tight-fitting jeans. O'Reilly couldn't help but marvel at how the unusual outfit showed off her full figure and ample breasts.

'Steady on there, detective,' she smiled. 'I'm only wearing this because I was fast asleep below when your partner demanded our services.'

Geraldine rooted around in the drawers at the rear of the wheelhouse and found an old Aran sweater. Pulling the heavy garment over her head, she tied up her long auburn hair in a ponytail. She approached the instrument panel and began fiddling with the buttons.

The wheelhouse was spacious and well equipped for such a dilapidated trawler. It boasted a functioning instrument panel, a Decca Navigator and Decca Track Plotter, as well as a laptop computer connected to a host of sensor devices.

'Don't worry. It's a calm night, so we should have a smooth crossing.' Geraldine drank some of her coffee and then switched on various machines and devices.

'Hang on and I'll go down to help them get us underway,' she smiled again as she left the wheelhouse.

When she opened the door, the cold air hit O'Reilly like a hammer. The wheelhouse had seen better days, but at least it was warm. Through the window, O'Reilly could see Chalkie pointing towards the harbour. The skipper wrapped himself in his coat and put on a pair of gloves to protect his hands.

Dykes jumped onto the pier and untied the two ropes that secured the boat. He threw the ropes on the deck and climbed back on board. After securing the ropes, Chalkie went aft, pulled a large lever embedded in the deck and listened as the anchor rose from the seabed. He had one last look around, sniffed the sea air and directed Dykes to the wheelhouse.

'Jaysus, that's a cold one,' Chalkie shouted as he followed Dykes inside.

'Are you alright there for a while?' Dykes asked O'Reilly. 'We're just going downstairs to put on some dinner.'

The thought of dinner made O'Reilly queasy.

Dykes watched as his partner turned the colour of a shamrock.

'I didn't sign up for this,' said O'Reilly.

'I'd never have guessed.' Dykes laughed. 'Maybe you should stay in Galway and monitor the investigation from the squad room. I'm beginning to think you shouldn't have wolfed down your dinner so quickly.'

Just then Geraldine returned and offered to make more coffee.

O'Reilly sat up straight in his chair and tried to look excited. 'I'm raring to go.'

'Don't worry about him,' Geraldine said, unconvinced by O'Reilly's newfound vigour. 'I'll take good care of him. If you two leave us alone, I'll have us in Kilronan in no time.'

When Chalkie and Dykes went below, the young detective sat in silence as Geraldine did some last-minute checks and fired up the engine. She switched on the iPod that was sitting on the dashboard and 'Fisherman's Blues' by The Waterboys blared out of the speakers.

She gave the engine a minute or two to warm up, dancing to the rhythm of the music as she waited, and then she eased the old diesel engine into action. She lit up a marijuana cigarette as she steered the trawler around the docks and guided her out to sea.

O'Reilly didn't know whether to arrest her or marry her.

9

IN THE field next to Ivor's Pub were half a dozen shipping containers with the words 'Hapag-Lloyd' blazoned across the sides of them. That's where Marcus was headed when he exited the back door of the pub and walked across the yard.

Marcus stepped through a hole in the wall and into the adjacent field. Standing outside the door of the nearest container was a mountain of a man wearing a classic black tuxedo and wellington boots. The outline of several tattoos could be seen through the fabric of his white shirt.

'How's business tonight, Fintan?' Marcus asked as the bouncer held the door open.

'No bad, Father,' Fintan said in a thick Glasgow accent. 'It's chokers in there and no mistake.'

'Good man, Fintan.'

'Watch your step, Father.'

'Just call me Marcus,' the priest said, stepping into the container and onto a plush carpet.

The inside of the containers was filled with gaming tables. Each container housed a different section of the casino, with doorways cut out of the metal walls to allow easy access to each section. The walls and ceilings were

covered with ornate decorations designed to make visitors
feel at home. It looked for all the world like a Victorian
brothel. The bar area and the cashier's cage took up one
container, and the others housed tables of roulette,
blackjack and poker. All the gaming tables were manned by
croupiers wearing matching black shirts.

Marcus walked up to the roulette table and smiled at
Debbie Durkin, who was counting out chips for a recently
successful gambler. Debbie smiled back and handed
Marcus a large notebook. The priest took off his leather
jacket and opened the notebook. He browsed through the
last few pages and signed the last one, making sure to note
his arrival time.

The casino had been in operation for about a year, and
Marcus had held a middle-management position from the
beginning. Ivor had come up with the idea one day after
he'd returned from a trip to Amsterdam. He'd known of a
casino in Dublin that had gone bankrupt and was prepared
to let him have the gaming tables for a good price. From
his time in Las Vegas, Ivor knew there was money to be
made in casinos, especially if he didn't have to bother with
a gaming licence or pay any taxes. The shipping containers
had washed up on the beach one day and Ivor had hauled
them across the island. He was hoping for another one to
make an even set.

Marcus made a mental scan of the room and watched as
Ivor came in carrying a tray of chips. The nightly poker
session was about to start, and Ivor always officiated over
that himself. Marcus hated Wednesdays. Every Wednesday,
the island's unemployed collected their dole money and
many of them spent the afternoon at Ivor's pub, followed
by the evening at the casino.

Marcus wiped the smile off his face when he spotted
Jimmy Roberts approach.

'How's it going, boy?' Roberts smirked at him.

Marcus shuddered when he heard the man's grating North of Ireland accent. He didn't know much about Jimmy, but he knew enough to steer clear of him.

Jimmy was tall and lanky with a hint of acne on his pale face. His stiff frame and arrogant smile betrayed the air of superiority that most Ulster Protestants seemed to display when they encountered Irish Catholics. In the short time he had been on the island, Jimmy made life hell for everybody he encountered. He looked out of place in such a stylish casino with his black Adidas tracksuit bottoms and hooded sweatshirt. The inner-city effect was completed by the hoodie draped over his head.

Marcus nodded reluctantly as Jimmy came closer to the roulette table. 'Are you flying solo tonight, Jimmy?'

'That's the little woman over there,' he said, pointing at an angelic creature sitting at the bar wearing attire similar to Jimmy's. 'I think you know her, as a matter of fact.'

Marcus knew who Lucy Shannon was and why she was in the casino. He couldn't make out everything he said because Jimmy was missing most of his front teeth, but he wasn't going to go through the anguish of getting him to repeat himself.

'Probably better than you.'

Jimmy studied the roulette table and sat down on one of the empty stools.

'I thought you were barred.' Marcus regretted saying the words as soon as he had uttered them.

'Well, you see, I have money tonight. So, your boss wasn't as reluctant about letting me in.' Jimmy placed five hundred-euro chips on the table. He put a hundred-euro chip on the 'street' containing numbers one, two and three. Debbie spun the wheel and flicked the white ball onto it.

She stretched her hands out above the table and moved them in a waving motion.

'No more bets, please.'

The ball bobbled. It hit one of the numbered slats and jumped. It bounced from number to number and came to rest on thirty-five.

'Black thirty-five. Odd.' Debbie placed a crystal marker over the winning digits.

She scooped up Jimmy's chip and allowed it to fall down a chute into a drawer under the table. Jimmy stared at Marcus and repeated his bet. Debbie spun the wheel again.

'No more bets, please.'

Jimmy watched as the ball jumped from slat to slat and finally landed on number sixteen.

'Red sixteen. Even.' Debbie took away the chip and repeated the action. Jimmy placed the same bet as Debbie flicked the ball onto the spinning wheel.

'No more bets, please.'

The ball landed on number two.

'Black two even,' said Debbie.

A hint of a smile appeared on Jimmy's face. Debbie placed the crystal marker on number two and then put ten one-hundred-euro chips in front of Jimmy, who let the previous bet ride. Debbie spun the wheel again.

'No more bets, please.'

The ball landed on two again.

'Black two. Even.'

Debbie placed ten more hundred-euro chips in front of Jimmy, who threw a hundred-euro chip back on the table. Debbie picked up the chip, tapped it on the table a few times to indicate it was a tip and placed it in the tip box at the side.

'Not bad for a day's work, is it Marcus?' Jimmy said, placing his winnings in his pocket.

'You were lucky tonight,' said Marcus. 'Don't spend it all in the same shop.'

'Anyway,' Jimmy looked pleased with himself, 'we have a wee business proposition for you.'

Marcus was surprised it had taken him so long to get to the point.

'I don't think I would be interested.'

'How do you know if you haven't heard it?'

Marcus ignored the question and watched as Debbie flicked the ball on the spinning wheel.

'No more bets, please.'

'We're going to find Willie's still, you Fenian bastard, whether you like it or not. And when we do, we're going to destroy it. Then what'll you do?'

Marcus wasn't stunned to discover Jimmy's plan—or rather, Lucy's plan. He knew Lucy was about to start a poteen operation on the island and intended to broaden her horizons. If Lucy's goal was to be the sole distributor of poteen in the west of Ireland, as he suspected, he and Willie were the only people standing in her way.

'I told you already, I'm not interested,' said Marcus.

'That's no way to talk to a potential partner, is it lad?' Jimmy left his stool and stood in front of Marcus.

They watched as Lucy approached.

'You're not causing a fuss, are you, Jimmy?' Lucy said. 'I wouldn't like to think you were upsetting the staff.'

Marcus hadn't had a run-in with Lucy for a while. She lived on the mainland and seldom returned to the island. He had been glad to see the back of her, but he knew she often came back whenever she was on the run from the Gardai. Local gossip suggested Lucy's trips to the island had become more frequent. Now he knew why.

He could see right away that she was the brains of the operation. Under a certain light, Lucy could have been a presentable woman. She had shoulder-length blonde hair and a confident air. With her slight frame, she seemed to be the female equivalent of her boyfriend. It didn't look like she cared much about her appearance and she seldom bothered with makeup or any other cosmetic niceties. Her only gesture towards femininity was a flower-patterned hair band.

'He's being a prick, darling,' said Jimmy. 'He seems to think he's better than us.' Jimmy sat back down again and took out a stool for Lucy.

'Is that true, Marcus? Do you think you're better than us?'

Lucy's piercing grey eyes bore into Marcus's soul and sent shivers down his spine. He felt more uncomfortable in her presence than he could ever remember feeling with anybody else. She had a disturbing way about her that seemed to permeate the atmosphere in the casino.

'He's got big ideas for a small man,' Jimmy said. 'He thinks he's great just because he's a priest.'

'Shut up and piss off over to the bar like a good man,' said Lucy, sitting down. 'Give me some of those chips in your pocket.'

Jimmy did as he was told and moved away as Lucy took her place at the roulette table.

Marcus had known Lucy for all of her twenty-one years. She was a problem child, and she'd grown up to be a problem adult. The fact that she was the only daughter of Marcus's oldest and dearest friend just made matters worse.

Right from the start, Lucy had been impossible to control. She had constantly got into trouble at school, and it had always fallen to Marcus to straighten her out. Since her father wasn't in the picture, Marcus had taken it upon himself to be the child's father figure.

When she was twelve, Marcus had arranged for her to enter Kylemore Abbey, a Catholic boarding school for girls in Connemara. He'd assumed the Benedictine nuns would not only educate her but also realign her moral compass. It had also been his hope that her temporary relocation would give her mother some peace and quiet.

By the time Lucy had turned eighteen, though, she'd become incorrigible. She'd failed her Leaving Certificate exams and spent six months at a detention centre for wayward women. Neither Marcus nor Sarah had seen much of her after that, and when they did, it always meant trouble. Marcus had had to admit defeat and resign himself and her mother to the fact that Lucy was beyond rehabilitation.

Lucy placed a chip on black and watched as Debbie spun the wheel.

'We're a bit concerned about your poteen operation, Marcus. You see, we were thinking of getting into the same lark.'

There it is, thought Marcus, *straight from the horse's mouth. They're starting their own poteen business.*

'No more bets, please.'

The ball landed on number sixteen.

'Red sixteen. Even.'

Debbie grabbed Lucy's losing chip. Marcus would have preferred to be almost anywhere else in the world at that time than sitting across from Lucy Shannon.

'We want to know where that English friend of yours keeps his still, and we want a list of his customers,' she continued, as Jimmy returned.

Marcus was proud of their poteen business and he'd be damned if he was going to lose it to a couple of bullies. He was able to put away money every month for the church, so he wasn't going to give it up without a fight.

'How many chips do you have, Jimmy?' Lucy shouted across the room.

'The guts of two grand, love.'

'Give them to me.'

'What? All of them?'

'Give them to me.'

Jimmy made his way back over to the table and placed twenty-four one-hundred-euro chips in front of Lucy, who arranged them in two piles and placed them on black. Marcus nodded at Debbie and watched as she flicked the ball onto the spinning wheel.

'No more bets, please.'

Lucy rose from her stool as the ball danced from slat to slat. It landed on sixteen again.

'Red sixteen even.'

Lucy banged her fist on the table as Debbie placed the crystal marker on the correct number, shovelling Lucy's chips down the chute.

Lucy's face turned red with rage as she screamed at Marcus. 'Do as I say or I'll rip your church apart, brick by brick.'

The casino was stunned into silence. Embarrassed, Lucy sat back down again and smiled in the general direction of the other gamblers.

'Now look what you made me do, Marcus. I've made a holy show of myself.'

Marcus thought he had handled himself well under the circumstances, and he was surprised when Jimmy's fist hit him square on the jaw.

The casino fell silent again when Marcus flew backwards on his chair, hitting the floor. Before he realised what was happening, Jimmy was standing over him. Jimmy reached down and lifted Marcus off the ground, throwing him across the floor.

Marcus crashed into the wall and let out a helpless groan. Jimmy was over Marcus again, but before he could renew his attack, Marcus was able to sit upright and punch Jimmy between the legs.

As Jimmy buckled with the pain, Marcus stood up and punched him in the head. He approached Jimmy and wrestled him to the ground. He pinned him there for a second before Lucy pitched in and raised a bottle above her head. She was just about to smash the bottle over Marcus's head when Ivor appeared out of nowhere and grabbed her around the neck.

Lucy dropped the bottle and began kicking her feet to break free. Ivor had a firm hold of her, but he was unable to prevent her from kicking out at the gaming tables and the other patrons. Finally, he let her go and watched as she fell to the ground. Before she could get up, he caught her arm and held it behind her back. She kicked her legs back and her left heel managed to connect with Ivor's shin. He grimaced in pain and let her go.

Marcus turned his attention back to Jimmy, who was still spread-eagled on the floor. He grabbed Jimmy, swung him from side to side and then threw him against the wall. Jimmy was levelled on the floor and in no condition to retaliate.

Having got the better of Ivor, Lucy once again picked up a bottle of beer and raised her arm to fling it at Marcus. The priest managed to gather his strength and kick Lucy kung fu-style in the head. Ivor regained his composure and seized the bottle, pinning Lucy's arm behind her back. He grabbed her in a headlock and took a firm hold, guiding her towards the exit. He kicked the container door open and dragged her across the field.

When Fintan, the bouncer, was made aware of the situation, he kicked off his wellington boots and entered the fray. As he ran toward the action, he took off his tuxedo jacket to reveal bristling biceps covered in Celtic tattoos. In his sleeveless shirt and bare feet, he looked for all the world like the Incredible Hulk in mid-transition.

Jimmy appeared concerned by the approaching bouncer, whose tattoos seemed to have much the same effect on him as a crucifix on a vampire.

Fintan gripped Jimmy around the shoulders and the taller man offered little resistance when the bouncer slammed him against the wall. Jimmy bounced off and hit the floor with a thud. When Fintan came up behind Jimmy and placed his arm around his head to get him in a headlock, Jimmy couldn't resist the opportunity to bite one of his tattoos. He picked a tattoo that depicted the Irish tricolour flag and bit into the green with the only four remaining teeth in his head.

The bouncer's face was contorted in agony as he tried to pull his arm out of Jimmy's mouth. Marcus grabbed a beer bottle and used the top end to pry Jimmy's mouth open. They finally freed Fintan's arm and they could only watch as the blood spurted out at all angles. Fintan ignored the pain—he grabbed Jimmy in another headlock and shepherded him towards the door.

Jimmy reached out and held onto the doorframe in a last-ditch effort to gain the upper hand. He turned around and growled at Marcus, who was on his feet and dusting off his clothes. 'You better wise up, boy, or you'll find yourself in a world of trouble.' His voice tapered off as Fintan hauled him outside and chucked him down beside Lucy.

Marcus wasn't afraid of Lucy, but he was none too pleased about having publicly humiliated her. Lucy was vindictive and could rear her ugly head sometime in the future when Marcus least expected it. When he got his wind back, Marcus walked over to the bar.

Ivor smiled at Marcus. 'I suppose you'll be wanting a pint?' he said, as if nothing had happened.

'I will,' said Marcus, 'when you're ready.'

10

THE waves were crashing against the *Aran Angel* as the ancient trawler laboured towards Kilronan Harbour. Chalkie and Dykes were sitting in the galley, enjoying the spaghetti bolognaise Dykes had just made. They listened to the weather forecast on the radio as Dykes poured each of them a glass of 2006 Rocca di Montegrossi.

Chalkie savoured the wine and then dug into the spaghetti.

'Ah, nice choice, my friend. You can't beat a Chianti Classico.'

'You certainly can't.' Dykes and Chalkie clinked their glasses and downed another mouthful.

'What's the story with this new yacht of yours?'

'I had a look at her on Tuesday evening at the docks, and I put down a deposit.'

'Where did you get the money? I thought Anna cleaned you out.'

'She did. But I hid a nice sum put away for a rainy day.'

'But you don't know anything about yachts.'

'I know enough to get by. I was in the Sea Scouts, you know?'

'You don't just turn on the engine and steer her where you want to go. You have to know how to arrange the sails, and you have to be able to navigate.'

'You remember that time I caught you coming into Malahide Harbour with a boat full of cigarettes and booze? We boarded your boat, and you were too drunk to steer.'

Chalkie burst out laughing. 'You had to steer us in while I sat behind you, and the other guard had to work the throttle.'

'We nearly ran into a super-yacht worth two hundred million euro, as I recall.'

'That's what saved me in the end. Your bosses in Harcourt Street were so busy counting the cost of the damage you caused that they ran out of steam.'

'Imagine what they'd say if they knew you were my brother-in-law at the time?'

Chalkie swallowed another mouthful of spaghetti and smiled.

'How is your sister, by the way? Is she still with that bastard Proinsias?'

'Proinsias knows a good thing when he sees it. What he did to you was disgraceful—now he has your wife, your house and your money. I'm glad you kept some cash on the side.'

'That's what I'm using to buy the yacht,' said Dykes.

'I think she only married you because she was impressed that you were on Mary Robinson's close protection detail. She thought she could go with you on all those trips abroad.'

'What? You mean those romantic getaways to Rwanda and Belfast?'

'I'm glad I didn't buy your MG convertible from Anna. I wouldn't give her the pleasure.'

Chalkie saw the horrified look on Dykes's face and decided to change the topic. 'Right, I'll do the dishes if you bring your niece up her food and check on the young lad.'

Dykes scooped a helping of spaghetti bolognaise into a bowl and left the galley.

O'Reilly's stomach churned with every wave. He raced for the door and made it just in time to throw up all over the wheelhouse steps. He narrowly missed his partner, who was on his way up to join them.

'You better come down on deck for a while.'

Geraldine held out her hand to grab the bowl of spaghetti bolognaise from Dykes.

'Thanks, Uncle Jim,' she shouted.

Dykes held his partner by the arms and guided him down the steps. The young detective felt better once he started breathing fresh air. The air was cold, but it was better than the sickening smell of diesel and marijuana on the bridge. O'Reilly eased himself to the side of the boat. He rested there for a while and leaned over the side.

Dykes stood beside his partner and tried to keep his balance. The boat swayed from side to side as the waves splashed onto the deck.

'How are you getting on with the skipper's daughter?'

O'Reilly looked up at the wheelhouse. 'She's a bit too modern for me, sir.'

'Did you smoke any of her pot?'

'Certainly not, sir.' O'Reilly stood to attention as he spoke.

'At ease, detective. You're allowed to let your hair down every now and then.'

O'Reilly stared at the water. 'You and Barbara,' he said. 'Is there anything going on there?'

'What?'

'Garda Barbara Casey.'

'What about her?'

'Is she a free agent, or are you shifting her?'

Dykes laughed and slapped O'Reilly on the back.

'Take my advice and stay away from women. They're nothing but trouble.'

O'Reilly lifted his head just as a mighty swell hit him in the face and nearly knocked him off his feet.

'She called you "Uncle Jim",' he said, recovering. 'What's that all about?'

'You're as sharp as a tack, you know that?'

Dykes eased himself away from the railing and made his way down to the galley. O'Reilly followed a step behind. He tried to walk faster, but the movement of the boat prevented it.

They descended the steps to the brightly lit galley and Dykes rejoined Chalkie at the dining table.

'You better lay down a while, lad,' said Chalkie, pointing at one of the bunk beds at the far end of the cabin.

O'Reilly groaned. He wondered if he'd ever set foot on solid land again.

II

Marcus thought about his precarious position as he sat in the living room with a bag of ice balanced on his aching face. He was sorry he'd let things get this far, and he knew he had to resolve the situation before it got worse. He allowed his mind to wander as he relaxed in his comfortable armchair.

The living room at the Nees' farmhouse hadn't changed since Marcus was a boy, except for the television in the corner of the room. It was Marcus's favourite place to relax, and it was more comfortable than his quarters at the rectory. He shuddered at the thought of living there next to the dilapidated old church with its leaking roof and crumbling walls.

He remembered what the church had been like when he was growing up. It had been a magical place, full of excitement and potential. He and Sarah used to visit the church grounds regularly, helping Father O'Flaherty with the gardening or with odd jobs around the place. The old priest used to regale them with ancient stories from the Bible, sowing the seeds for a lifelong passion that would provide Marcus with a rewarding vocation.

But Inis Mór had a large congregation in those days, and Father O'Flaherty always had plenty of money to pay for the upkeep of the building. The number of island residents had dwindled since then, and Marcus had always struggled to pay for the constant maintenance that the church needed. He resented the fact that the Archbishop of Tuam had forced him to resort to more unorthodox methods of making money. He decided that if he ever got back to Rome, he would pull strings at the highest level to make sure the parish got all the funds it needed.

Now he also had to worry about Lucy and consider what she might do to get her hands on his poteen business. But it wasn't just the poteen operation he was worried about— it was the actual physical damage she might inflict on his friends.

Marcus was awakened by the sound of barking.

'Pipe down, you dirty mongrel,' Eamon shouted.

Marcus opened his eyes to the sight of Eamon standing over him with a cup of tea in his hand. 'What are you going to do about Lucy? Can't that mother of hers do anything?'

'I don't want her mother to get involved,' Marcus took the cup from his father. 'But I've got Gilligan on the case to make life a bit more difficult for Lucy.'

He took a sip of tea and watched as his father sat down on the sofa.

Just then, the barking got louder and the doorbell rang.

Marcus looked at his father, who was pretending not to have heard the chime.

'You're a lazy sod,' Marcus growled as he got up to see who was at the door.

Marcus opened the door and was surprised to find Willie standing in the cold night air. He opened the door wider and invited him in.

'Hope I'm not interrupting anything, dear boy. I was just passing and thought we might have a chat.'

Marcus smiled and gestured for Willie to follow him into the kitchen.

'Come in,' said Marcus. 'The old man just made a fresh pot of tea.'

'Ah, nothing like a late evening beverage,' Willie smiled and sat at the kitchen table.

The Englishman waited as Marcus poured the tea.

'I have some discouraging news for you, Willie.' Marcus grabbed a magazine, rolled it up and used it to encourage Judas to vacate the last remaining kitchen chair.

Willie looked concerned. 'What's wrong?'

'Lucy came into the casino with her boyfriend,' Marcus said, sipping his tea. 'We had a bit of a barney. They mean to shut us down and start their own business.'

'That doesn't come as a complete surprise, dear boy. What did you say to them?'

'Nothing. I told them to feck off and then we started fighting.'

Willie poured milk into his tea, added sugar and stirred. He took a sip of his tea as he shifted his gaze to Marcus.

'We should think about moving the operation to the mainland,' Marcus said, pouring himself more tea. 'It's only a matter of time before they find the still.'

Willie looked troubled as he grabbed his mug from the table. 'There was something I was meaning to tell you.'

Marcus waited as Willie struggled to find the right words.

'I've come to a rather important decision and I was waiting for the right time to tell you.'

'Spit it out, for Christ's sake,' said Eamon, who had been listening from the doorway.

'I was thinking about retiring.'

'What do you mean, "thinking about retiring"?' asked Eamon.

'Get out and mind your own business,' Marcus shouted at Eamon. 'Don't you think that's a bit hasty, Willie?'

'I was thinking of doing a bit of travelling—see the world, that sort of thing. I know it's a bit sudden, old boy.'

'Are you doing this because of Lucy?'

'Not at all, dear chap. Although, she may have hastened my decision. The fact is, I'm getting too old for bootlegging. I'm afraid the long trips and inclement weather are getting the better of me.'

'But you're as fit as a fiddle.'

'I'm afraid not,' Willie replied, reaching down to touch his knees. 'I've had a touch of the gout for some years now, and the cold weather is playing havoc with it.'

Marcus and Eamon were stunned into silence.

'Well, that beats all.' Eamon walked over to the coat rack and picked up his jacket. 'I'm off out for a walk, Marcus, while you talk some sense into him.' He put on his jacket, opened the door and braced himself for the cold.

'You better not be going to the pub!' Marcus shouted as Eamon closed the door behind him.

Willie took another sip of his tea and looked at Marcus. 'There's been another development I have to tell you about.'

'Don't tell me—you've decided to convert to Catholicism.'

Willie fiddled with his fingers for a moment.

'Jesus, it's like getting blood from a stone,' Marcus sighed.

'Well, you see, I've met someone. She's fabulous and I think I'd like to settle down with her.'

'That's fantastic. Do I know her?'

'I'd rather not say, if you don't mind. I haven't popped the question yet.'

'Your secret is safe with me.' Marcus raised his cup of tea to toast Willie.

'I have a friend who owns a hotel in Italy. A seaside town called Sperlonga, halfway between Rome and Naples.'

'Yes, I know it well,' said Marcus. 'We used to go down there when I was at the Irish College in Rome.'

'He wants me to invest in the place and be an equal partner. The lady in question loves Italy, and I think she'd fancy moving there—for a while, at least.'

Marcus smiled and drank another mouthful of tea.

'It's a quiet town with only around three thousand people. The beaches are fantastic and there's enough tourism to make a go of the hotel. The weather is great and it's close enough to an airport if we need to leave in a hurry.'

Willie waited a moment to gauge Marcus's reaction. 'My friend has just lost his partner to cancer and he has rather fallen apart. It would be just as much a humanitarian mission as a business one. I've been brushing up on my Italian and the boat is as good as sold.'

'*Tutto e bene quel che finisce bene.*'

Willie thought about that for a minute and decided he needed more Italian lessons. 'I might have a solution to the Lucy problem.'

'How do you mean?'

'We could lure Lucy to the still and have Gilligan and a few other people there waiting for her. That would get Lucy out of our hair and then the business could continue unimpeded.'

'I don't think Gilligan would be up to it. Besides, I don't want too many people knowing the location of the still.'

Willie took a sip of tea and wiped his mouth with the back of his hand. He looked at Marcus. 'You're not vexed with me for giving up, are you?'

'Of course not,' said Marcus. 'You deserve your retirement—we'll muddle along without you. We might even come and visit you if you give me a discount on the room.'

Willie and Marcus looked at each other and smiled.

11

I T WAS just after ten at night when the *Aran Angel* entered Kilronan Harbour and drifted towards the pier. It had turned into a clement night, but the two police officers had had quite enough of boats for now. The cloudless sky was glistening with stars, and the moon was almost full. The boat rocked a bit as it glided across the bay. Geraldine White steered the craft into the pier and moored her next to the numerous other boats.

She switched off the engine, left the wheelhouse and made her way aft to join Dykes. Chalkie helped Dykes onto the pier and then threw him a rope, which Dykes grabbed and tied to the pier. Geraldine called out to O'Reilly, who seemed reluctant to leave the wheelhouse and face the cold. With a little coaxing, Geraldine helped him onto the pier and waited for Dykes to grab hold of his partner. Once the detectives were on firm footing, Dykes untied the rope and threw it back into the boat.

'Can I have your phone number?' O'Reilly asked Geraldine.

'I'll call you,' she said, keeping a wary eye on Dykes. 'I can get your number from Uncle Jim.'

O'Reilly looked dejected as Geraldine and Chalkie went through the motions of casting off again. Geraldine went back to the wheelhouse and switched on the engine. Dykes threw the rope back onto the boat as the vessel eased away from the pier.

The boat was a few metres out from the pier when O'Reilly let out an unmerciful roar. Chalkie stopped what he was doing and looked up to investigate the cause of the commotion.

O'Reilly was standing on the pier, pointing at his red duffel bag, which was still lying on the deck of the boat. Chalkie growled as he grabbed the bag and threw it onto the pier at O'Reilly's feet. The young officer retrieved the bag and threw it over his shoulder. When he turned to join his partner, Dykes was already making his way up along the pier towards the village.

'They better be tasty sandwiches, lad,' Dykes shouted. 'That's all I can say.'

Kilronan was a small village by normal standards, but it was the largest on Inis Mór. It contained several guesthouses and pubs, a youth hostel, a souvenir shop selling Aran sweaters, a bicycle rental shop and a supermarket.

Right in the middle of the village was a stone Celtic cross that had been erected by the local people to commemorate the life of Father Michael O'Donaghue, a priest and island benefactor from the time of the famine. Just behind that was a large grey building that housed a pub called The Bar.

The two detectives were tired as they approached the Pier House guesthouse, which was right between the village and the dock. Dykes felt cold and miserable, but he had to concentrate on the matter at hand.

'Right, you go in there and check us in,' Dykes said, pointing at the two-storey cream-coloured building. 'Meet me over there at The Bar when you're finished.'

O'Reilly followed the lane to the guesthouse as Dykes carried on towards the village. He could just about make out the sound of music and chatter coming from the local pub.

The Bar had several sections, each with its own special function. The main bar catered to locals and didn't offer much in the way of comfort. The lounge, which was at the back of the building, was preferred by tourists because it had a pool table and a telephone. The front yard also doubled as an ample drinking patio, which the owners optimistically referred to as a beer garden, complete with wooden benches and seats.

When Dykes arrived, the beer garden was full of patrons struggling to keep warm as they puffed the life out of their cigarettes. It always amazed Dykes that the smoking ban had given birth to a new breed of drinker who was willing to endure freezing temperatures just to enjoy a smoke.

The police detective walked through the main door of the building into the pub, which was full of old men wearing tweed caps and tourists in brightly coloured jackets. The volume of their conversations seemed to hush to whispers as Dykes walked across the room and settled into an empty space at the counter.

'What can I do you for?' said the portly man behind the bar.

'I'm looking for Geraghty,' Dykes said.

'Who's looking for him?'

When Dykes introduced himself, Rory Geraghty stopped wiping the beer glasses and leaned against the counter in front of the detective. He was a middle-aged man with the look of somebody who had something to hide.

'That's me,' said Geraghty.

Dykes presented his warrant card and snarled. 'I'd like to ask you a few questions and buy a toasted ham sandwich.'

Geraghty shrugged his shoulders to indicate he could arrange the ham sandwich but wasn't so sure if he could answer any questions.

Dykes sat on a stool and took off his coat. After ordering a pint of Guinness, he told Geraghty he was looking for the man who had passed the five-hundred-euro note the previous morning. Geraghty's mood seemed to improve when he realised the detective wasn't investigating any crimes he might have committed.

'I remember the man, but I haven't been on the island long and don't know many of the locals.'

'Can you describe what he looked like?'

'That's the funny thing.' Geraghty topped off Dykes's pint and placed it on the counter. 'He was bald, but he also had long hair. And he had a funny accent.'

'What kind of accent?'

'English, I think. He was posh, but he was dressed like a knacker.'

'What do you mean?'

'He was all *la-di-dah* and proper—all *old man* this and *dear boy* that. But he didn't look like he had a pot to piss in. I mean, apart from the five hundred euro.'

Dykes didn't think it would be too hard to find someone who matched that description.

'How old was he?'

'He was in his late sixties at least,' Geraghty guessed. 'But he had a fierce red face. I'd say he wasn't afraid of a drink or two. He polished off a bottle of wine while he was here.'

Dykes took a sip of his Guinness and studied Geraghty for a moment.

'You didn't get his name, I suppose?

'I did not.'

Dykes drank some more of his stout and unfolded the sketch of the suspect that Brady had drawn. He showed it to Geraghty.

'Is this the man?'

'Yes, that's him. But he wasn't wearing a baseball cap.'

Dykes smiled and watched as his partner walked in through the door, accompanied by another reduction in conversation volume.

'Better make that two toasted ham sandwiches.'

II

Eamon had taken off his artificial limb and had long since grown weary of waiting for Father O'Flaherty to open the sacristy door.

'Maybe he changed the lock,' the old priest said.

'No, he didn't. He would have told me if he had.'

Eamon shifted on the doorstep to stop his posterior getting numb and dropped the flashlight in the process.

'Here, let me have a go.' He grabbed the keys from O'Flaherty and positioned himself to get a good look at the keyhole.

O'Flaherty picked up the flashlight and switched it on. As the beam of light hit the ground outside the sacristy door, O'Flaherty couldn't help but notice Eamon's artificial leg. He picked it up and examined it. He was amazed to discover that the inside of the plastic limb was hollow.

'Is this what they mean when they say drinkers have hollow legs?'

'What?' Eamon was still struggling with the lock. 'What are you sayin' to me?'

Eamon turned around and glared at O'Flaherty.

'Gimme that back, you feckin' eejit!'

O'Flaherty pulled away as Eamon tried to grab the leg. The one-legged man frowned as he turned his attention back to the lock.

'I keep forgetting—you're completely useless without this.' O'Flaherty had a wicked, mischievous grin on his face.

Just then, both men heard a click from the lock and the door swung open.

'Go in there and fill up that leg with holy water bottles, like a good man.' Eamon moved to the side of the step to allow O'Flaherty access.

'Why should I?'

'Look at me. I can't walk. You wouldn't begrudge a sick man a few bottles of holy water, would you?'

'You're a sick man, alright. And I'm sick of you.' O'Flaherty stepped over Eamon and entered the sacristy.

Eamon watched as the old priest opened the large wardrobe at the side of the room. His eyes opened wide with delight as he saw all the Virgin Mary-shaped holy-water bottles sitting on the shelves of the wardrobe. O'Flaherty grabbed a chair and placed it in front of the wardrobe. Easing himself onto the chair with a groan, he began filling the hollow leg with holy-water bottles. When it was full, he placed a couple of bottles in his coat pocket. He lifted the leg and brought it over to the back door, where Eamon was waiting.

'You're a decent man, do you know that?' Eamon accepted the leg and grabbed one of the holy-water bottles.

He opened the lid and tasted the contents.

'Ah, that's more like it.' He put the bottle back in the leg and began the process of reattaching it to his stump.

O'Flaherty helped Eamon lift himself up off the ground and watched as he tried to keep his balance.

'Aren't you forgetting something?' he said as Eamon attempted to walk up the laneway.

Eamon stopped in his tracks and put his hands in his pocket. He took out a set of silver rosary beads and handed them to O'Flaherty.

'Have your beads back—one good turn deserves another.'

'A good turn, is it? You're nothin' but a bloody rogue.'

O'Flaherty closed the sacristy door as Eamon carried on up the lane.

12

THE Bar was heavy with the smell of whiskey and stale beer as the late-night patrons finished off their last orders. It should have been closed hours before, but neither the bar staff nor the patrons showed any signs of leaving. The locals had little incentive to go home because they had no reason to get up early in the morning. Geraghty had knocked off for the night and left the glass cleaning duties to his young apprentice, who was glad of the work.

Lucy and Jimmy were sitting at a corner table, engrossed in conversation with Geraghty. Lucy couldn't believe her ears as Geraghty regaled her with his tale of stolen money and detectives hot on the trail of a fugitive bank robber.

'How much money?' Lucy Shannon asked under her breath.

'One point eight million,' said Geraghty.

'Is that so?' Lucy sent Jimmy off to secure a round of drinks.

It took Geraghty only a few minutes to give Lucy all the information. She listened to everything she was told, but she tried not to appear too interested. It wouldn't do to give Geraghty the impression the information had any monetary value to her.

It didn't take Lucy long to figure out that Geraghty's description of the bank robber bore a striking resemblance to Marcus's English partner. She realised there was a good chance Willie was in possession of the stolen money. It was also possible that Marcus knew all about the money because he and Willie were friends.

But she had to be careful. She knew Geraghty didn't know Willie, and she wanted to keep it that way. She also had to make sure the police would never find the old man. And the only way to make sure of that was to find him first and send them in the wrong direction.

Lucy believed finding Willie would give her an opportunity to kill not two, but three birds with one stone: she could put a stop to his poteen operation, take the stolen money for herself and get her own back on Marcus.

Ever since she'd been a child, Father Marcus Nee had ruined her life at every turn.

She blamed him for talking her mother into sending her to a convent where she'd spent the unhappiest six years of her life. Kylemore Abbey was a beautiful castle situated in one of the most picturesque locations in Connemara; however, to Lucy it was a prison run by a group of psychopathic nuns who had made her life a living hell. Just after her twelfth birthday, she'd been shipped off to that Catholic 'Borstal' and had stayed there until the age of eighteen. She had been forced to live with over two hundred other girls, most of whom were just as treacherous as she was, and she'd only been allowed home for Christmas and the summer holidays.

She had tried everything to escape her fate—she'd broken every rule in the hope of getting expelled, and even run away a few times. But each time she'd thought she was free, Marcus had been there to whisk her back to school and comfort her mother.

Even during the summer holidays, Marcus had given her no peace. He had forced her to work when all the other teenagers had been out having fun, and he'd made her give most of her wages to her mother. She'd done stints working as a barmaid, a shopkeeper, and even for a while as an assistant at the bicycle rental shop. When she'd tried to make extra money on the side, Marcus had usually been around to scupper her plans. He'd made her work for no wages for two months one summer to pay off Mattie Dwyer for the two bicycles she'd sold on the mainland.

Marcus had spoken on her behalf during her trial at the Galway Criminal Court, but she'd still been sentenced to six months for robbing an off-licence in Galway city. She suspected he'd only spoken in court to please her mother and that he had been responsible for her conviction. She'd had plenty of time in Loughan House in County Cavan to plan her revenge.

If there was ever a chance to make life uncomfortable for Marcus, Lucy considered it a moral imperative to make it happen.

After her release from the detention centre, she had stayed away from Inis Mór and put as much distance between herself and Marcus. She remained in Galway city, where she'd met Jimmy and eked out a meagre income robbing houses. When she has saved enough money, she moved further west to Connemara to set up her own poteen business.

'I know who the bank robber is,' Lucy told the barman at last. 'And there might be something in it for you if you could introduce me to your new friends.'

Geraghty's eyes lit up. He knew the guards would be mad at him for interfering, but he was sure they would welcome whatever information he brought their way.

'I think that could be arranged.'

II

O'Reilly found himself sitting on the church steps, admiring the moonlight as it glistened on the wet street and the stone walls. After leaving the pub, he had gone for a walk to collect his thoughts before retiring to the guesthouse for the night. As Dykes was in a foul mood, O'Reilly didn't fancy accompanying him back to their accommodations. And now here he was, sitting on the church steps.

He didn't consider himself a religious man, but he did go to Mass every Sunday and on holy days, out of obligation. His mother was religious, of course, and O'Reilly always liked to please his mother.

As he sat there, he thought about the last few days and the path he'd taken to becoming a detective. He had been trying to become a good detective, but it was a matter of great concern to him that he was falling down on the job. Of course, it didn't help that he had a gruff mentor, who was being booted out of the job, and obtuse colleagues who didn't respect him.

He knew he hadn't covered himself with glory by getting sick on the boat and giving Dykes the opportunity to excuse him from the investigation. But the senior officer should have considered that it was his first time on a boat.

He heard a door closing in the church behind him. Glancing at his watch, he wondered who would be up at that hour. It was nearly midnight.

He turned and saw an ancient-looking man limping his way towards him with the aid of a walking stick. The old man was wearing a heavy coat, but O'Reilly could just about make out the priest's collar.

O'Reilly rose to attention and raised his arm to help the old man down the steps.

'You're a considerate young man,' Father O'Flaherty said as he accepted the detective's arm. 'Did you want to get into the church?'

'No, Father, I was just sitting here thinking about life.'

'You don't want to do too much of that, young man. You'll end up more confused.'

'Do you have far to go, Father? Can I give you a hand?'

'No, stay where you are. I'm just going across the *boreen* to the parochial house.'

O'Reilly sat back down on the steps again and smiled at the old-timer.

'Are you on holidays?' the priest asked.

'I'm not really sure what I'm doing here.'

'That makes two of us.' Father O'Flaherty studied the detective for a moment. 'Plenty of fascinating people have sat where you're sitting contemplating life, you know? The novelist Liam O'Flaherty, no relation, was born not far from here and the playwright John Millington Synge published a journal about his time here.'

He rummaged in his pockets and took out two Virgin Mary-shaped holy-water bottles, which he handed to O'Reilly.

'Are these any good to you?'

'Thank you, Father.' O'Reilly accepted the little bottles and placed them beside him on the steps.

The old priest turned around and limped across the *boreen*. O'Reilly continued watching as he opened the gate and disappeared down a winding path. O'Reilly looked at the bottles and picked one of them up. He opened the lid, sprinkled a little on his finger and did the sign of the cross.

'That's not going to do much good,' he said to himself.

He raised the bottle to his mouth and drank some of the contents, inducing a fit of coughing and spluttering.

'What the hell...?' He took another sip and decided he liked the taste.

III

Eamon didn't know how long he'd been sleeping on the back doorstep of The Bar. He looked at the three empty holy-water bottles on the ground beside him and estimated it might have been a while. He remembered being escorted out the back door of the pub by an irate barman.

Picking up his prosthetic limb, he checked inside to make sure there were plenty of holy-water bottles left. He attached the limb and began the process of standing upright.

Eamon located his bicycle leaning against the stone wall, but it took him a while to mount it. When he finally climbed on, it took him even longer to get the hang of it; he zigzagged along the road as he careened down the hill into the village.

He could hear someone singing in the distance as he picked up speed. He knew he was going too fast, but he was unable to remember at that precise moment in time how to engage the brakes.

'*I met my love by the gasworks wall.*'

The singing was getting louder, and Eamon could see he was on a collision course with the vocalist. He clipped him hard, swinging him around a full three hundred and sixty degrees, and then carried on down the hill towards the waterside.

'*Dreamed a dream by the old canal.*'

He closed his eyes as the bicycle bore him over the concrete lip and into the soft sand below. He landed without incident, but he could still hear the singing.

'*I kissed my girl by the factory wall.*'

He reached for his prosthetic limb to fetch another bottle of holy water, but the limb was nowhere to be seen.

IV

O'Reilly was having a whale of a time, even if he was nearly knocked over by a crazy fool on a bicycle. He was singing and dancing and even tried to climb the Celtic cross in the centre of the empty village.

'*Dirty old town. Dirty old town,*' he sang at the top of his voice in a tone that could only be described as grating.

He had a feeling his actions were wildly inappropriate, but he decided he didn't care. Unzipping his fly, he proceeded to urinate along the base of the Celtic cross.

'*Clouds are drifting across the moon.*'

The detective was surprised and pleased in equal measure when he noticed more holy-water bottles scattered on the ground next to a prosthetic limb. He opened one of the bottles and drank the contents in one satisfying gulp.

Noticing lights being switched on in several windows around the village, he increased his vocal range so everyone could hear. He felt gratified when he saw a ginger-haired clown approaching him at speed, followed by a buxom woman.

The singing detective closed his eyes and waited to accept their adulation. He imagined himself crooning in a large auditorium accompanied by the cheers of thousands of screaming fans.

'*Cats are prowling on their beat.*'

The red-haired clown was getting closer as O'Reilly raised his arms and blew kisses to his fans. He felt a sharp pain at the top of his head and his eyes were filled with a bright light as he fell to the ground with a thud.

'You get his feet, Fidelma, and I'll take his head,' were the last words O'Reilly heard before the lights went out.

THURSDAY

13

MARCUS allowed the gentle wind to caress his face as he took in the view before him. He seldom ventured up to the roof of the church, but when he did, he always enjoyed the vista. To the south across Galway Bay, he could see all the way to County Clare and to the north the rocky expanse of Connemara.

He could see the local Gaelic football team training on the nearby GAA pitch. Admiring the playing field, he wondered how they managed to carve out such an even rectangle of lush, green grass out of the harsh landscape of rocks and bog. Players from all three islands made up the one Aran Islands team, and it was Inis Mór's turn to host the twice-weekly training session. Despite its small pool of players and lack of funds, the club had had some success in the Galway Junior Football Championship.

Since it was such a balmy morning, Marcus had decided to mend some of the slates on the rickety old roof. After assessing the areas that needed the most work, he rearranged the slates accordingly, using a hacksaw to cut them to fit. It was a laborious, time-consuming process, but it allowed Marcus to think about other things.

The state of the roof reminded him how much he still had to do to bring the church back to its former glory. A few euro here and a few euro there was no good in the overall scheme of things. He needed something big to get the money rolling in.

He had considered the idea of putting on a massive rock concert and wondered if he could get Bono or Bob Geldof on board. Then he thought about a television telethon with Marty Morrissey as the host and a line-up of celebrity guests.

Producing marijuana or cocaine might be going too far, he thought, even though Rock Island provided plenty of privacy for such endeavours. It hadn't been so long ago that Marcus had considered poteen to be beyond the pale and he hoped the day would not come when he would say the same about cocaine. He decided it would be unwise to add drug trafficking and distribution to a list of questionable activities that was getting longer by the week.

Lighting a cigarette, he looked out at the ocean for inspiration. Maybe God would send him a sign, or better yet, maybe the money would just materialise out of thin air.

When he was finished fixing the roof, he put the last of the broken slates and the other materials into his bag. He was just about to dismount his perch on the ridge of the roof when he heard a melodic voice coming from below.

'Permission to come aboard?' Sarah Shannon was already at the top of the ladder when Marcus turned around.

'Be careful there. It's not safe.' Marcus admired Sarah's legs as she made her way up the side of the pitched roof to the top. She placed a leg on either side of the ridge and sat next to Marcus.

'I can never get enough of this view,' she said as she opened her canvas bag. She took out a cold bottle of Heineken and handed it to Marcus.

'You remember when we used to come up here as kids?' she asked, using her cigarette lighter to open her own bottle.

'O'Flaherty was never happy to see us up here,' said Marcus. 'But he never told our parents.'

Marcus opened his bottle using the same cigarette lighter and took a sip of beer. He studied Sarah's face as she stared off into the distance.

'Is everything okay with Willie?' Sarah asked at last.

'Have you heard something?'

Sarah nodded her head and sipped her beer. 'What do you know about his activities in Galway?'

'He doesn't tell me a lot. Why?'

Sarah looked at Marcus as she took another sip. 'It's just that Lucy has got it into her head that Willie has stolen money from a bank in Galway.'

'That's ridiculous. Where did she get such a crazy idea?'

'Two Special Branch detectives are here chasing a bank robber. They just arrived last night.'

'What's all that got to do with Willie?'

'Lucy thinks Willie matches the description the guards have of the robber. She's convinced he stole the money and hid it somewhere on the island.'

'That means he's in danger.'

'I know,' said Sarah. 'Have you seen him?'

'He came to the house last night,' Marcus said. 'Did you know he has decided to quit the business? And he's fallen for a woman.'

'Is that good or bad?'

'I think it's a good idea. He wants to move to Italy with her.'

'Let's hope he can stay away from Lucy until this whole mess is sorted.'

'What were the names of those two guards?'

'Laurel and Hardy, Lucy said.'

The two friends admired the view as they drank the last of the beer. Marcus turned his head when he heard Sarah sobbing.

'What's the matter, pet?' Marcus put his arms around her and she rested her head on his shoulder.

'Did I make a terrible mistake, Marcus?' Sarah sobbed. 'All those years ago in Dublin—I know I made a terrible mistake.'

'What do you mean, Sarah?'

'I'd been waiting for you to ask me to marry you and then I got pregnant. I wanted to terminate the pregnancy before you found out, but you knew straight away. That evening when I came home from the doctor—' she stopped talking and began sobbing louder, recovering after a moment. 'I knew you wouldn't let me have an abortion once you found out and that was the end of us. I knew we couldn't be together after that and I had to come back here.'

'Hush now, that's all water under the bridge,' Marcus whispered. 'We've been together most of our lives, haven't we? We've had a good life, the pair of us.'

Sarah continued sobbing. 'I ended up with nothing. Lucy is an ungrateful criminal and I ended up dating a long line of drunken, wife-beating bastards. I should have had you, and then I would have been happy.'

A light drizzle started to fall as Sarah lifted her head. She dried her eyes with the sleeves of her coat and tried to smile. 'You are the love of my life; did I ever tell you that?'

'Many times—in fact, you never shut up about it.'

They both laughed as Marcus packed up the last of his tools. He gestured to Sarah that they should leave their lofty nest.

'I have to hear confessions in five minutes,' Marcus waited for Sarah to ease herself down the slope of the roof and onto the ladder.

Just then, one of the Aran footballers was attempting a free kick from near the halfway line. Marcus watched as the player settled himself and then ran towards the ball. He kicked it with a mighty thud and kept it in sight as it sailed over the bar.

'You know, we might just win the Junior Championship this year.' Marcus smiled as he made his way down the ladder.

Margaret Sheridan had been the church cleaner for most of her adult life. She found it easy to combine her duties at the church with her 'real job' at the post office because, in reality, she did little work in either place. Her main purpose in both jobs was the acquisition and timely dissemination of gossip, an activity in which she excelled.

She had fond memories of Father O'Flaherty in his heyday and even Father O'Brien before him. But she had her doubts about the young Father Nee. He was far too modern and trendy for her liking.

She was well into her sixties, but her hips were strong and she moved around with the speed and agility of a woman half her age. Her height and weight were average, though she had a large rear end so out of proportion with the rest of her that it often inspired unkind comments. She tried to hide her dimensions by wearing long quilted coats of the dark green variety favoured by people who enjoy shooting pheasant and cross-country horse riding.

Margaret wasn't pleased when she looked out the church window and saw Marcus kissing Sarah Shannon on the cheek.

Disgraceful behaviour, she thought, *and right in front of God's house.* She had known the two of them as children and watched them grow up. They'd always been thick as thieves, and there was no telling what they got up to behind closed doors. The whole parish was aware that they'd spent a long time together in Dublin years ago and that Sarah came back with a baby.

And then he had returned a few years later to become a priest, bringing with him his new-fangled ways. He was a nice enough fellow, she supposed, but she wouldn't let him hear her confession.

When Marcus walked in the front door of the church, he smiled as Margaret scampered away from the window and grabbed her broom. He glanced across at the half-dozen villagers who were waiting near the confession box.

'I'll be with you in a second,' he shouted across the church.

Margaret pouted when he walked up to the altar and started rummaging around the tabernacle. She got a good look at his tattered jeans and bare feet and shot him a disapproving stare.

'That's odd,' Marcus said, turning to Margaret. 'The tabernacle key is missing. Have you seen it?'

'That depends, Father.'

'On what?'

'On what a tabernacle is.'

'You don't know what a tabernacle is? How long have you been coming to this church?'

'I only work here, Father. I can't be expected to know what's in every nook and cranny.'

115

'It's the chamber to the rear of the altar where we keep the sacred host.'

Margaret looked at the priest and then looked over at the tabernacle.

'Is that what it's called?

'Well, have you seen the key?'

'It was here yesterday because I remember cleaning it and putting it back in the keyhole. But it's not here now. One of them tourists probably came in and took it. You shouldn't keep the church open 'till all hours, you know?'

Marcus frowned and walked towards the back of the church where the confessional box was situated. Margaret put away her sweeping brush and followed him.

'I'll keep an eye out for it, Father.'

Marcus dismissed her with a wave as he approached the waiting sinners. Looking around, he noted it was always the same people every day—they waited all morning to confess the same dreary trespasses and then they went out and did the same all over again. He chastised himself for wishing that, just once, one of them would have a juicy transgression to impart. It would be refreshing to live in an ungodly environment like Los Angeles, London or Ballinasloe, where the faithful lived iniquitous lives that better facilitated the perpetration of immoral activities.

He opened the door of the confession box and stepped in.

The segmented booth was a dark, unyielding tomb where even the most pious of creatures were apt to unleash their guilty secrets. Marcus sat on the padded chair in the middle compartment and waited for one of the doors to open. As he expected, the door on the left opened at the same time as the one on the right. Margaret up to her old tricks, he thought.

'You're not supposed to be in here during confessions, Margaret,' Marcus bellowed. 'I thought we discussed that.'

'Sorry about that, Father,' she said as she crept back out. 'I was just giving it a little clean.'

'I don't know why you bother—the bloody walls are soundproof and you can't hear what anyone is saying.'

He waited for Margaret to close the door behind her before he placed his holy stole over his head. He made the sign of the cross and slid open the screen at the side.

'In the name of the Father, and of the Son, and of the Holy Spirit. Amen.'

'Bless me, Father, for I have sinned,' said a male voice on the other side of the screen. 'It has been a day since my last confession.'

Marcus knew from the voice that it was Mattie Dwyer. He sat back in his chair and braced for the onslaught. 'What are your sins, my son?'

'Times have been hard, Father, and I haven't been renting any bicycles. I have mouths to feed and I had no choice.'

'What did you do, my son?'

'It started off with one every now and then—there was no harm in it, Father.'

'No harm in what, my son?'

'And then I was forced to escalate, you see?'

'Escalate what, my son?'

'It was just too easy and I couldn't stop—two, three sometimes four at a time. I even brought my youngest, little Iggy, for moral support.'

'Oh, for goodness sake, spit it out, man,' Marcus shouted, losing his patience.

'The chickens, Father.'

'What about the chickens?'

'I stole them, Father. 'Stankard's chickens.'

'You stole Stankard's chickens?' Marcus was relieved to get to the bottom of the mystery. 'John Joe Stankard's chickens?'

'Yes, Father. We'd go in through his top field in the dead of night. We'd sneak into his yard and they'd be just sitting there. We'd throw them into sacks and off we'd go. I told my auld wan I bought them.'

'Why haven't you confessed these sins before? You're in here every day and there hasn't been a peep about chickens.'

'I've been working up to it, Father.'

'Well, you'll have to stop. I'll be monitoring the situation to make sure you've stopped.'

'How will you know I've stopped, Father?'

'I'll start counting Stankard's chickens to make sure they don't continue disappearing.'

'Sure, I'm not the only one who's taking them. Stankard has a hundred chickens up there and the lads are stealing them all the time. You won't tell Gilligan, will you?'

'I can't tell Sergeant Gilligan. You're protected by the seal of the confessional.'

'That's good then.'

'Tell me who else is stealing the chickens.'

'I can't do that, Father.'

'Why not?' Marcus asked, exasperated.

'They're protected by the seal of the pub.'

Marcus buried his head in his hands and resisted the urge to scream. He found himself wondering how Mattie managed to run after so many chickens and not lose his hideous toupee in the process. He smiled at the thought of some poor chicken wandering around Stankard's yard with Mattie Dwyer's toupee draped over its head.

'For your penance, I would like you to recite fifteen Hail Marys and twenty Our Fathers. And I want you to tell those other chicken thieves to come in here and confess their sins. Is that clear?"'

'It is, Father.'

'Now, recite the Act of Contrition while you contemplate your sins.'

'Oh my God, I am sorry for my sin with all of my heart. In choosing—'

Marcus had enough to worry about without having to protect Stankard from chicken thieves. He resolved to figure out a way to notify Stankard of the problem without breaking the seal of the confessional.

'—suffered and died for us. In His Name, my God, have mercy.'

'God the Father of Mercies, through the death and resurrection of His Son, has brought forgiveness of sin to the world,' Marcus muttered. 'Through the ministry of the Church, I grant you pardon and absolution for your sin in the Name of the Father, and of the Son and of the Holy Spirit. Amen.'

Marcus made the sign of the cross. 'You may go in peace.'

'By the way,' he added before Mattie opened the door. 'You didn't happen to see the tabernacle key anywhere, did you? Since you seem to be inclined towards thievery, I cannot assume your criminal appetites have not evolved beyond chickens.'

Mattie kneeled again with a heavy sigh. 'What the hell is a tabernacle, Father?'

'It's the chamber to the rear of the altar where we keep the sacred host.'

'Oh, is that what it's called? I've always wondered about that. I thought you kept money in there or something.'

'Well, have you seen it or not?'

Mattie thought about it for a moment. 'I have, Father.'

'When?' Marcus nearly jumped out of the box with excitement. 'When did you see it?'

'On Sunday, Father. At mass. When you used it to open the tabernacle.'

Marcus couldn't get angry at Mattie. He knew the man had neither the intelligence nor the sense of humour to be funny. The poor sod thought he was being helpful.

'A minute ago you didn't even know what a tabernacle was.'

'Ah, but I know now what it is,' said Mattie. 'And I have one of them—what d'ye call them—photography memories.'

'Get outta here, like a good man, and send the next one in.' Marcus lowered his head in disappointment as Mattie opened the door and left.

14

DYKES was refreshed after a good night's sleep, a hot shower and a shave. He'd enjoyed a decent breakfast at his guesthouse and then walked it off with a stroll along the pier and back up to the village. He sauntered into The Bar and smiled when he saw the amber turf fire blazing in the fireplace.

Even if he wasn't happy about having to investigate this ridiculous robbery, he was glad to be in Aran, away from the daily drudgery of his life. He knew he'd have to go through the motions of doing some work, but that could wait until after his coffee. He resolved to get it over with and enjoy the fresh air in the process. There were aspects of the case he wanted to discuss with O'Reilly, but he was unable to locate him all morning.

When Rory Geraghty appeared out of nowhere and placed a piping hot mug of coffee in front of him, Dykes's thoughts drifted and he was away in another world.

'What did I do to deserve such efficient service?' Dykes lifted the coffee mug to his lips.

'I was hoping to put you in a good mood,' said Geraghty.

'I was in a good mood before you spoke and now I'm edging toward anxiety. Have you seen my partner?'

'I haven't seen him, but I have friends who have some information you might be interested in. I was just telling them about your mysterious bank robber, and they think they might know him.'

'Where are these friends of yours?' Dykes asked, looking around the bar.

'Not so fast,' Geraghty smiled. 'I was wondering is there might be some sort of reward.'

'It depends on the information.' Dykes tried to resist the urge to put his hands around Geraghty's neck and throttle the life out of him. 'Take me to your friends.'

Geraghty walked out from behind the bar and opened the side door. 'Follow me.'

Dykes grabbed his coffee, rose from his stool, and followed Geraghty out to the beer garden.

When they stepped through the main door onto the front terrace, Dykes was glad he was wearing his overcoat. He braced against the bitter cold as Geraghty led them to a garden bench occupied by a man and a woman who were wearing matching tracksuit bottoms and hoodies.

'Were you out jogging?' Dykes inquired, referring to their clothes.

'What?

Dykes was amazed by young people who wore sportswear in cold weather, even when they weren't engaging in sporting activities. It was popular among drug dealers, he observed, probably because it allowed them to run faster when pursued. If he'd met these two loitering in Galway city, he would have arrested them on the spot.

'You know the man we're looking for?' Dykes asked the woman sitting on the bench.

'We *might* know him,' said Lucy Shannon.

The detective tried to prevent the anger from showing on his face. This woman seemed to be in a position to co-operate with the gardai in a robbery inquiry, but she wasn't being co-operative. He didn't like the look of her either, and he assumed she had fractured a law or two in her time.

'Do you know him or don't you?' He was struggling to hide his impatience as he sat down on the bench opposite Lucy.

Lucy leaned back on the bench and smiled. She stubbed out her cigarette in the ashtray, causing the ashes to fly around in all directions.

'His name is William Shuttleworth-Banks. He runs an illegal poteen operation with the local priest. Find the priest and you find your bank robber.'

'Is that right?' Dykes said, barely able to keep the sarcasm out of his voice. He stared at Lucy.

'That's right.'

The detective sergeant was wary of unsolicited information. 'I don't know who you are. Why should I trust you?'

'I can assure you, officer,' Lucy leaned forward on the bench, 'I have no reason to deceive you.' She got up from the bench and gestured to Jimmy to do the same. 'I'm just trying to help. You can take it or leave it.'

Dykes held Lucy by the arm.

'There's no need to be like that, is there?' he said. 'Let me get you a drink.' He looked at Geraghty, who was still standing nearby, and made a gesture with his fingers instructing him to fetch a round of drinks.

Lucy sat back down again and pouted in Dykes's direction, pretending to be offended.

'Don't be angry but, I have to ask—why are you being so helpful? What's in it for you?'

'Let's just say our interests are temporarily aligned. If you arrest the pair of them, I could take over their poteen operation.'

Dykes thought about that for a moment as Geraghty returned with two hot coffees and a bottle of beer.

'Where does he live?' Dykes asked.

'I don't have that information,' Lucy picked up her coffee mug and drank. 'If I did, I'd go there myself instead of telling you about it.'

'A noble sentiment, to be sure. But how do I know you're telling the truth? You could be lying just to get rid of a rival.'

'Well, why don't you investigate? That's what you were trained to do, wasn't it? If I were you, I'd start with the priest.'

Lucy stood up and waited for Jimmy to drink his beer.

'Oh, by the way,' she said to Dykes. 'You'll want to visit the Garda Station. Sergeant Gilligan has something of yours.'

Dykes watched as Jimmy and Lucy walked down the stone steps to the main road. Geraghty scurried over and stood in front of Dykes.

'Did you get what you needed?'

'Mind your own business.' Dykes downed his coffee and kept his eye on Jimmy and Lucy as they carried on down the road.

Jimmy struggled to keep up with Lucy as she walked down the hill toward Cockle Strand.

'Why are you helping him find the money?' Jimmy asked.

'He won't find the money—he'll be too busy interrogating Marcus. That will give us enough time to find Willie and get the money.'

'How will we find Willie?'

Lucy looked at Jimmy and smiled. 'I haven't figured that out yet.'

Lucy didn't know where Willie lived, but she could keep the police busy while she looked for him. She knew the Garda detectives represented a potential obstacle to her plan, but she intended to turn that to her advantage.

'What do we need, Jimmy?'

'I dunno,' said Jimmy. 'What do we need?'

'We need guns—and I know where to get them.'

About an hour later, Dykes left the pub and made his way to the Garda station. He wondered where his partner had disappeared to, but the fact that he could move a lot faster without him wasn't lost on him.

He walked at a steady clip, passing several tourists on the way.

When he entered the station, Dykes was amazed at how small it was. The main office and the public area were divided by a counter that went from wall to wall. The public area was no bigger than an ATM vestibule and had no furniture apart from a few scattered chairs. The walls were covered with the usual crime prevention posters, some of them decades old.

Dykes was able to see all the way to the back of the station, where the holding cell was located. As amazed as he was with the size of the station, he was even more surprised to see his partner and fellow detective sitting next to an old drunk in the holding cell.

'O'Reilly, what the fuck are you doing in there?' Dykes shouted.

The senior detective could feel the anger welling up inside him as he watched an old lady rise from her desk in front of the cell and approach the counter.

'You'll have to keep the noise down now,' she said.

'Is Gilligan around?' Dykes shouted.

'Not at the moment. Can I take a message?'

With that, a middle-aged man with ginger hair and an enormous pot belly waddled in from an adjacent room. He was wearing a string vest and seemed to be drying his hair with a towel.

'It's alright, Fidelma. I'll deal with this.' He approached the counter and looked at Dykes. 'I'm Sergeant Gilligan. What's all this shouting about?'

Dykes took out his warrant card and introduced himself. 'I'm Detective Sergeant Dykes. Do you usually conduct police business in your undergarments?'

'Does he belong to you?' Gilligan asked, pointing to O'Reilly.

'Yes, he does. And I want him back.'

'I'm afraid that's not possible. He is to be remanded in custody until the Aran District Court convenes next week.'

'You must be joking. Why is he here?'

'I never joke about the Aran District Court. It's not a matter for levity.'

Gilligan wrapped the towel around his neck and picked up his notebook from the desk. He consulted his notes for a few moments and read, word for word, what he had written the previous night.

'The accused will be charged with disturbing the peace, indecent exposure, attempted murder and resisting arrest. On the night in question at approximately half-past two in the morning, the accused was singing and dancing abroad at the Celtic Cross. He unzipped his fly and inebriated—

sorry, urinated—on the said statue. In full view of Fidelma, I might add.'

'Attempted murder,' O'Reilly shouted from his cell. 'Who did I attempt to murder?'

'I think that was me, Sean,' said Eamon, who was sharing the cell with O'Reilly. 'I hit the ground fairly hard when you knocked me off the bicycle.'

Dykes opened the thick telephone book on the counter and flicked through the pages.

'He knocked down a handicapped man on a bicycle and nearly killed him. He woke up half the island with his singing and the dogs were barking for hours afterwards. The accused continued singing even after he was incarcerated in his cell, and Fidelma couldn't get to sleep for a long time after that.'

'Let him out, Gilligan,' Dykes tried again.

'That Celtic Cross was erected by the local people to commemorate the life of Father O'Donaghue. It has survived stampedes of rampaging cows, violent storms and even English soccer hooligans on stag parties. And it nearly came down last night at the hands of that fat little gurrier.'

'I've been trying to lose weight,' O'Reilly said from behind bars.

Gilligan's monologue was interrupted when Dykes picked up the telephone book and hammered him in the face with it. Gilligan was knocked off balance, but he managed to remain standing.

'Ah, there's no need for that,' Fidelma screamed.

Dykes reached in over the counter and grabbed hold of the towel around Gilligan's neck. Using both hands, he tightened the towel around the sergeant's neck, causing Gilligan's face to get redder than it already was.

'Look into my eyes, Gilligan,' Dykes whispered.

Gilligan did as he was told as Dykes tightened his grip. 'Yes, yes,' he repeated.

Alright, you made your point,' Fidelma said, placing the keys on the counter.

Dykes let go of the towel, allowing Gilligan to fall in a heap into the chair behind him. When he regained his breath, Gilligan shot Dykes a disapproving stare. 'Fair enough,' he grabbed the keys off the counter. He shuffled over to the cell and opened the door for O'Reilly.

'You can go now,' he said to O'Reilly. 'And you can stay where you are,' he said to Eamon, who was already standing, ready to leave.

'Ah, come on, sergeant, have a heart.' Eamon watched as O'Reilly shuffled out and Gilligan closed the cell door behind him.

'We'll discuss this later,' Dykes said to his partner when they were reunited.

'Did you see my red duffel bag, sir?' O'Reilly asked.

'No, I did not.'

'Where did I leave the fuckin' thing?'

'It'll turn up. In the meantime, you can do without your sandwiches.'

Dykes watched as O'Reilly loaded up his fork with half a sausage, half a tomato and a rasher, putting the whole lot into his mouth. The young officer chewed for a moment, swallowed and washed it down with a mouthful of tea.

'Hungry?' Dykes inquired.

'I deserve a decent breakfast after my ordeal. That was hard time.'

'Hard time? You were only in there a few hours.'

'Why aren't you eating?' O'Reilly pointed at the slice of pizza in front of Dykes.

Dykes looked down at the pizza and picked off a piece of fruit, holding it in front of O'Reilly's face. 'Pineapple has no business on a pizza.'

From their vantage point in The Bar's beer garden, Dykes could see the whole village and the harbour. He breathed in the fresh air as a gust of wind rustled the map of Inis Mór spread out on the table in front of him.

'Incarceration gives you an appetite, you know? You only start to appreciate your freedom after it's been taken away for a while. You took your sweet time getting me out, by the way.'

'I didn't know where you were,' Dykes explained. 'Anyway, I was busy investigating.'

'What did you find out?'

'I got a tip from some of the locals,' Dykes said, 'but I need some more information to put the tip into perspective.'

As O'Reilly ate his breakfast, Dykes explained what Lucy had told him. He acknowledged that Lucy might have been lying through her teeth, but he couldn't tell fact from fiction. He had to consider her information before making his next move.

'It's my contention that she thinks she can have all the money for herself if she sends us in the wrong direction,' Dykes said.

'Maybe you should just take her at face value and look for the priest.'

'That's what she wants us to do. If the priest was going to be any help, she wouldn't have mentioned him. We have to concentrate less on what she told me and focus instead on what she didn't tell me. We need to find the suspect, not the priest.'

'Isn't it funny how nobody knows where this character lives. I made a few inquiries around the village last night—

before my episode—some say he lives on his boat, while others say he lives on an isolated island.'

'These people would never cooperate with the Guards,' said Dykes, 'we're on our own.'

O'Reilly looked at the map and noticed that the southeast was more populated than the northwest. He suggested they split up and search each segment. But Dykes didn't like that plan and came up with one of his own.

'We might as well just get a jaunting car and search the whole thing together.'

Dykes could see from the map that the island only had one road. He used his finger to follow the road from one end of the island to the other.

'We'll start here in Kilronan, work our way northwest to Kilmurvey and Onaght and on to Bungowla. That way, we can cover half the island in one day.'

Dykes folded the map, downed the last of his coffee and laughed. 'I doubt if we'll get any help from Sergeant Gilligan.'

'What's a jaunting car?'

Dykes frowned at his partner as he put the map back in his pocket and stood up.

15

WILLIE had spent a lucrative night in Rossaveal selling poteen to the workers at the fish processing plants. The night shift clocked out at six-thirty in the morning, allowing him to sell the whole consignment before he returned to Aran. He got back to the yacht happy in the knowledge that he had done a good night's work.

As he pulled all the lines out of their cleats and off their winches, Willie's mind drifted to the events of the past few weeks. Life was about to change for him in so many ways that he couldn't even fathom all the details. He had fallen in love and they would soon be the proud owners of a romantic Italian hotel. Coming clean with Marcus about his retirement plans gave him some relief, but he had been reluctant to divulge the whole plan until everything was in place. Marcus wasn't just his business partner, he was also his friend, and he deserved to know everything. After all, he would soon inherit the poteen operation and all the headaches that went with it.

Willie let out the topping lift until the boom sagged downward and then he tied it again. He had a close call when the boom almost hit him as it swung around. He raised the anchor, switched on the motor and eased the vessel out of Rossaveal Harbour, keeping her pointed into the wind.

It was probably unusual for a man his age to find love, he realised. The thought of her radiant smile and the way the sun illuminated her blonde hair. She was only about ten years his junior, but she had the grace and vitality of a teenager.

They had met a few months before, on one of his trips to Galway city. He'd been loading supplies onto the yacht and she was at the docks waiting for a boat to take her to Kilronan. He offered to take her across on his yacht and, in return, she helped him with his supplies. On the voyage across the bay, they'd been amused to find they had several mutual acquaintances on the island. He found her not only attractive but also educated and outgoing. They shared a love for the poetry of Yeats and the music of Bob Dylan, and they were both passionate about Italian opera, food and wine.

She'd been excited about his plans to retire to Sperlonga, but disappointed that he'd have to sell his yacht to do so. That had been another thing they had in common. Since their first meeting, Willie had got to know her well, and yet he was surprised when they fell in love with each other. He would soon be ready to ask her to join him in his Italian paradise—he just needed to tie up a few loose ends and then he'd be ready to pop the question.

As he hoisted the sails, the thought of his new life filled him with trepidation and joy in equal measures. Looking around the boat, he admired his handiwork as both sails fluffed in the strong breeze. He continued to turn into the wind, tightening the sheets until they could go no further. The vessel was sailing a heading as close to the wind as Willie could manage, which was about forty-five degrees. The sea was restless and the wind was picking up as the vessel eased her way across Galway Bay.

As the sea whipped up, Willie began to wonder if he'd even make it back to shore. When the rain turned to hailstones and the visibility was reduced, he decided it was too risky to sail around to the dangerous inlets at Rock Island. He made up his mind to aim for the Nees' farm and hoped the yacht would at least get him that far.

The rain came down in sheets as he looked for a familiar landmass in the distance. He cursed himself for not paying more attention to the forecast and wished he hadn't ventured out so early. He was also beginning to regret not fixing the wiring issues he'd noticed earlier—he was afraid the deluge would short out his electrical systems.

He began to feel more optimistic when he looked to his right and saw the bright light of the lighthouse marking Kilronan Harbour. That wasn't where he was aiming, but now he had a fair idea where he was headed. As several familiar landmarks came into view to his left, he struggled to turn the yacht into the wind. He was relieved to discover that the boat was closer to shore than he realised. Keeping a close watch on the lighthouse at Straw Island, he guided the boat around it.

As he fiddled with the mainsail, he thought about his new business venture and the friend he hadn't seen for a lifetime. His plan was to use the money from the sale of his yacht to buy a forty-nine percent share in his old pal's hotel in Sperlonga.

The friend, Joseph Longshanks, had fallen into the depths of despair since the death of his boyfriend and the hotel, in consequence, had fallen into disrepair. Willie and

Longshanks, or 'Tattoo Joe' as he became known, had come down from Oxford together. They'd both shunned academia and drifted into the underground subculture of drugs and psychedelic music, squatting in a flat near Ladbroke Grove. When Joe was arrested for possessing cannabis in the late sixties, Willie took up his position at the British Natural History Museum and had never looked back.

Until he received a mysterious letter a few weeks before, the last he'd heard of Tattoo Joe was that he had become a roadie and gone to America with Pink Floyd. Joe had addressed the letter to the museum, which sent it to the post office box in Galway that Willie had given them as a forwarding address.

In the letter, Joe acknowledged that Willie had been the only person in the world he ever trusted. He described in detail the story of his life, how he'd seen and done everything a man could wish to see and do, covering his body in tattoos as he went. He had met and fallen in love with an Italian chef named Dominic and they settled in the only place in the world where they felt comfortable. He hoped that Willie was happy and successful wherever he was, but wondered if he might be of a mind to 'up sticks' and start a new adventure.

Joe described the 'boutique' hotel he'd bought in Sperlonga and the life he had shared with his lover. When Dominic died of cancer, Joe had lost all interest in life and had only recently plucked up the energy and the will to write to Willie.

The timing had been perfect as far as Willie was concerned. While he loved his life in the Aran Islands, he had become indifferent about bootlegging and saw Joe's offer as an opportunity to start anew. If he asked her nicely, he might even convince the new love of his life to join him in Italy.

As the inlet near the Nees' farm came into view, Willie thought about what it would be like to run his own hotel on the Mediterranean coast. He could speak only a smattering of Italian, but would surely become fluent with practice. His days could be spent concocting delicious Italian dishes and his nights enjoying cocktails on a sundeck watching the yachts on the Tyrrhenian Sea.

Once anchored, Willie lowered the sails by removing the tension from the lines holding them up. He folded the sheets and stowed them away in their bags on the deck, and then made his way downstairs to the cabin. He made a quick inventory and checked for rain damage. Satisfied all was well, he opened the door to his living quarters below deck and descended the short stairway into the darkness.

The chamber was flooded, and most of Willie's belongings were strewn across the floor. This didn't concern him too much because he knew the hull was intact and the water had come in from above. Rummaging through the debris, he tried to deal with the water. He grabbed a mop from a corner cupboard and started swabbing.

A loud noise that seemed to come from outside the boat startled him. Ignoring it at first, he thought it was the wind playing tricks on him. He turned his attention back to the floor.

Then there was another noise. Willie turned around to find a gaunt, dishevelled man standing in front of him, then noticed a set of shapely legs descending the steps. When the female intruder reached the lower deck, she seemed to be ignoring him. She appeared to be studying the décor, such as it was. Willie wondered why he was so popular all of a sudden. Putting his mop to one side, he smiled at his guests. He decided to introduce himself, but the woman spoke before he could get the words out.

'Take a seat, sir,' Lucy Shannon said without a shred of emotion. 'We have a few questions to ask you.'

Jimmy sat down on one of the cushioned seats along the side of the galley. With a loud grunt, he coughed up a mouthful of phlegm from the back of his throat and spat at Willie's feet.

'I say, what the bloody hell do you think you're doing on my boat?'

Ignoring the question, Jimmy walked through to the main compartment towards Willie. Without a word, he grabbed a clump of Willie's hair and pushed him down on one of the side seats. When Willie protested, Jimmy slapped him hard across the face, then backed away to sit opposite him. Lucy stared at Willie for a while and ordered Jimmy to tie him up.

Willie was too shocked to speak or protest when Jimmy bent over to tie a stout rope around his hands and legs. His victim bound, Jimmy leaned forward and punched Willie on the face.

'I think... I think you broke my nose,' Willie stuttered as blood poured down his face.

'And we might break a few more things before the day is out.' Lucy sat down again and lit a cigarette.

Willie was writhing in agony as he struggled to figure out what these animals wanted and why they were treating him like this. He racked his brain and tried to remember if he had ever met them before. As he sat there, bound and bloodied, he wondered what he could have done to upset them. 'We were wondering where you hid that nice bit of money you stole in Galway.'

Willie scrambled to find the words.

'I have no idea what you're talking about.' Willie tried to sound convincing but had a horrible feeling he didn't succeeded.

Sure enough, Jimmy reached over and punched Willie in the mouth. Lucy looked annoyed as she stood up to push her boyfriend away. She leaned down and looked Willie in the eyes.

'He's a bit of a bully, I'm afraid, my Jimmy,' she said. 'I don't think he believes you.'

Willie began to sob and wondered if it would do him any good to beg for mercy. He thought better of it when Jimmy took the cigarette out of Lucy's mouth, blew on the tip and rubbed it against the side of his neck. Jimmy was jolted backwards when Willie shuddered and screamed. Just before he passed out, she regained her composure and repeated the procedure on the other side of his neck.

Jimmy didn't know what the plan was, but he was sure the Englishman wasn't supposed to faint. He checked Willie's pulse and asked his girlfriend what they were going to do.

'Shut your mouth and untie him,' Lucy barked.

Jimmy did as he was told as Lucy climbed the stairs to the upper deck. He studied Willie for a minute and realised the old man was in a bad way. His nose was broken, and Lucy had given him two nasty neck burns. Jimmy was also sure he'd broken the Englishman's jaw when he'd thumped him.

Soon after, Lucy peered into the cabin and told Jimmy to bring the old man up to the deck. The morning was clear after two days of rain. It was cold, and Lucy's breath was a thick vapour when she exhaled.

'See that shed over there?' Lucy asked as Jimmy carried Willie up top. 'Drag him over there, like a good man, so we can have another go.'

Willie was in agony when he awoke about an hour later in a dark space. He was sitting on a wooden box and his hands and legs were bound with a liberal application of duct tape. Willie felt like every bone in his body was broken—and some of them were.

He looked around and saw that he was in the shed. He'd been there many times before and knew it was on the northwest corner of the beach. Ivor had built the shed several years before and used to store fishing equipment. But everyone knew Ivor also used it to entertain the occasional female companion, as evidenced by the empty wine bottles and used condoms scattered about the floor.

When Willie's eyes became accustomed to the darkness, he realised he wasn't alone; Jimmy and Lucy were also in the shed with him.

Lucy stood over the old man and lit another cigarette.

'Don't worry, pet,' she said as Willie shuddered. 'I only have one left and I'm not about to waste it on you.'

She bent over and examined the burn marks on Willie's neck.

'You're not being co-operative, are you?' she said.

Willie began to whimper. He waited for Lucy to inflict more pain, but she retreated, pulling up a box and sitting down in front of her victim.

'Why won't you tell us where the money is? It's no good to you if you're dead.'

She hated wasting time, and it dawned on her that that was what she was doing.

She wanted to find the money quickly because she wasn't sure how many other people were looking for it. Rising from the box, she decided to take the initiative and instruct Jimmy to fetch a pair of pliers from the toolbox.

Ordering him to sit down beside the Englishman, she resumed her position on the other side.

'Now, sir,' she said in a measured tone, 'you're going to tell us what we want to hear, or you're going to be sorry.'

Jimmy untied Willie's arms and grabbed hold of his left hand. He clasped the pliers around Willie's little finger and awaited further instructions.

'Tell us where the fucking money is,' Lucy shouted.

Willie panicked. He was in real trouble and he had to think of something. 'Listen, I have about two thousand euro in cash on my boat. You can have that. You can have all of it. Just let me go.'

Lucy nodded at Jimmy, who applied pressure to the pliers. Willie writhed in agony as the cold steel squeezed his finger and sent a torrent of pain through his body. He looked down and saw the blood spewing and his fingernail coming off.

'All right, all right,' he cried, 'I'll tell you what you want to know.'

Lucy moved closer to Willie and told Jimmy to keep the pliers in place.

She listened as Willie explained that he'd hidden the money underneath the poteen still behind his house. He said it was packed in a black sports bag and was easy to reach.

'Where's your house?' Jimmy was barely able to stand the excitement.

Willie tried to speak, but his head jerked back in an involuntary spasm. His face froze in a desperate expression of agony. Lucy watched in horror as Willie's eyes closed and his blood-soaked head fell limp to the side. She screamed when she saw what had caused the old man to faint. The steel pliers were still clasped around Willie's finger. Jimmy had used all his strength to inflict more pain than the victim had been able to bear. Gripped in the excitement of the moment, he had applied more pressure than was needed and caused the interrogation to end prematurely.

Lucy rose from her box and pushed her boyfriend away. He fell to the floor, but the pliers remained attached to Willie's broken finger. Lucy stood over her boyfriend and kicked him in the stomach with all the force she could muster.

'You fuckin' eejit!' she shouted. 'Now we'll never find the bloody money.'

FRIDAY

16

THE dark, grey sky was heavy with clouds, from which a dreary onslaught of rain and sleet continued to fall. Dykes and O'Reilly balanced themselves on the jaunting car and looked like a pair of miserable rag-and-bone merchants. They hunched down in their overcoats to shield themselves against the cold.

The horse tried to negotiate the muddy *boreen* without stepping into the treacherous minefield of puddles. As they approached the Nees' windswept farm, Dykes was still seething about what had happened to them the previous night.

As the detectives slept, someone broke into their rooms and stole their Garda-issue Walther P99 pistols. Apart from the embarrassment of allowing the theft to take place under their noses and having to report it to their superiors, Dykes was worried about being unarmed so far from home.

'We have to report it,' O'Reilly said, breaking the silence.

'No, we don't.' Dykes turned his head and spat onto the road. 'Losing your weapon or allowing it to be stolen is a sacking offence, especially if it happens at night when you're sleeping. Do you want to get sacked?

O'Reilly nodded his head as they continued down the road.

Suddenly, the horse stopped, lifted its tail, and proceeded to defecate all over the road. The hot, steaming excrement caused a foul odour, forcing Dykes and O'Reilly to block their noses.

'Jesus Christ,' Dykes said. 'What have they been feeding him?'

Dykes looked at the pile of shit as it splattered on the wet road. He was disillusioned about wasting a day and a half on a fruitless search and the accumulation of an endless stream of information that had yielded nothing more than sore feet and a growing disdain for the public at large. But they were on the right track now, he was sure, even if he questioned the dubious nature of the initial information that had led them there.

The experienced officer wasn't surprised they hadn't yet found the suspect. If his long, decorated career as a detective had taught him anything, it was that people would do almost anything to prevent the progress of an ongoing police inquiry. He reflected on the rebellious nature of the Irish people and felt it didn't bode well for the task at hand. For centuries, the Irish had fought against authority and the heavy hand of uniformed officials, primarily because those men in uniforms were foreigners who didn't belong. The Irish had lied, cheated and sometimes killed to protect themselves against the tyranny of their British oppressors. Even in the early days of the Irish republic, they'd found it difficult to trust the Irish-born police officers who were charged with their protection simply because they wore uniforms and embraced the ideals of the same British system they had fought to overthrow.

It was this determined defiance in the face of authority that had greeted the two Garda detectives as they'd searched for their fugitive. They'd visited almost every house on the southern tip of the island and were no closer to finding him. They had been wined and dined by farmers and innkeepers who were hell-bent on stymieing their progress. By the end of it all, they were drunk, tired and destined to return to Galway empty-handed.

'Do you mind telling me where we're going?' O'Reilly broke the silence when the horse finished its business and got moving again.

'I've decided to consider Lucy's suggestion.'

'What suggestion was that?'

'Who is the most important person in any rural Irish community?'

'I give up, who is it?'

'The priest,' Dykes looked at his partner as if he was a simpleton.

'The priest?'

'It'll be nothing more than another wild-goose chase, but it's worth a try.'

'Why didn't we go and see the priest yesterday when the weather was nice? You were told about him and you ignored the information.'

'That was a mistake, I realise that now,' said Dykes.

O'Reilly smirked at his partner as he guided the horse down the road.

II

Marcus was full of the joys of life as he walked along the *boreen* from the church to the centre of the village. He looked nothing like a priest in his faded jeans and wellingtons. Judas stayed a respectable distance behind, as if waiting for the optimum moment to pounce. The rain was coming down in sheets and visibility was poor. In the distance, Marcus spotted several tourists standing outside the Garda Station trying to open an umbrella in the strong wind. They lost the battle and could only watch as the wind caught the umbrella and sent it spiralling across the sky into the adjacent field. They ran toward the entrance to the Garda Station and took shelter in the doorway.

As Marcus made his way toward the Garda Station, he could just about make out what they were saying. He smiled to himself when he realised they were Italian. He heard one of them ask the others how the inhabitants managed to build so many stone walls. His companion wondered why there were no trees, and why there was nothing planted in any of the fields. Marcus also spotted Sarah, who had also taken advantage of the doorway's potential as a temporary shelter from the rain. He smiled as he approached the holidaymakers.

'*I campi sono pieni di pietre*,' Marcus said in fluent Italian.

The tourists looked at him in shock.

'*Lei parla molto bene L'italiano*,' one of them said.

Marcus smiled and nodded.

'That's why some of the fields can't be farmed and why there are so many stone walls— because the fields are full of rocks.'

The Italians seemed happy with the information, and one of them handed Marcus the map.

'*Puoi dirci dove siamo?*'

Marcus pointed to where they were and then to another area on the map. 'That's the famous Dun Aenghus prehistoric stone fort. If you hurry, you can make it there and back before it gets dark.'

The tourists thanked Marcus for his help as they folded up the map. The priest watched as they raised their hoods and made a dash for the pub.

Marcus turned and tripped over Judas, who had arranged himself under Marcus's feet. His face turned red with embarrassment as he looked at Sarah, who was sitting on one of the chairs in the doorway.

'You like showing off, don't you?' she said with a smile.

She leaned over and patted Judas on the head. 'I can't believe Judas is still alive. He was old when we were children.'

'He made a doggy pact with the devil,' Marcus said.

'He trips you on purpose, you know that?' Sarah smiled. 'He figures out where you are going and then he sits in front of you.'

Marcus returned her smile. He always thought Sarah had the most beautiful smile he had ever seen. He sat down beside her and eyed the rain. 'Have you no home to go to?'

'I was on the way home when I saw those two detectives heading towards your farm. I was just about to go over and tell you about it when the rain started.'

'Really? I wonder what they want with me. Anyway, I'd like to talk to them about Willie. I haven't seen him for a while.'

'Gimme a shout when you get some information—Lucy is more than likely looking for him as well.'

'I hope you didn't confront her.'

'She came to the house looking for clothes.'

'I've been wondering what her next move would be.'

Sarah gave Marcus a concerned look. 'Just be careful, okay?'

'I'll see you later.' Marcus rose from the chair. 'I have to go in and see this eejit about the missing tabernacle key.'

'The what?'

Marcus shot Sarah a look of despair as he opened the door and walked into the Garda Station. He walked up to the front counter and called out, 'Sergeant Gilligan? Gilligan, are you in there?'

Fidelma Lynch approached the sliding window with half a sandwich in her hand and the other half in her mouth. Even in the middle of eating, she looked agitated.

'Where is he? I have to report a robbery.'

'Who?'

'Gilligan.'

'Ah, the sergeant is out for his lunch. Robberies cannot be reported at lunchtime—Sergeant Gilligan is strict about that. Where did you say it was, Father?'

'Someone is after stealing the tabernacle key from the church.'

'What's a tabernacle, Father?'

'It's the box behind the altar where—,' Marcus stopped. 'Never mind that, just tell me where the bloody fool is.' Marcus saw no point in hiding his irritation any longer.

'Well, you'll have to fill out this form.' Fidelma presented the priest with three leaves of paper. 'And I'll need to see some form of identification.'

'What?' Marcus suspended his efforts to keep his voice down. 'You know who I am, don't you?'

'I do, Father. But rules are rules. Sergeant Gilligan is very strict about that.'

'Bloody woman,' Marcus mumbled under his breath as he turned to walk away. 'Tell him to give me a shout when he wakes up.'

'There's no need to take that tone, Father,' Fidelma said, taking another bite out of her sandwich.

III

When Dykes and O'Reilly neared the Nees' farm, they could see no sign of life. They descended from the car and approached the front door.

Dykes knew he wasn't handling the investigation with his usual gusto. He felt tired and uninspired, and he resented having to work so hard to spur himself on. Dykes was sure this was a waste of time and he feared they'd be treated to the same unnecessary kindness that had hampered their investigation thus far. He was in no mood to be cajoled and he resolved to quickly dispense with the usual pleasantries.

When he reached the front door, he knocked as hard as he could. O'Reilly peered in through a window and saw Eamon fiddling with his artificial limb.

'Jesus Christ,' O'Reilly exclaimed.

'What is it?' Dykes asked.

'I know who that is. That's Eamon from the jail.'

Dykes knocked on the door again and was greeted by a crooked-looking man with one leg.

'Do you know a man by the name of William Shuttleworth-Banks?' Dykes showed the old man his warrant card.

Eamon looked past Dykes and fixed his gaze on O'Reilly. 'Sean, how the feck are you? Come in out of that, lads. You must be freezing.'

Dykes wanted to stand his ground; however, his partner had already shuffled inside and he noticed an impressive fire blazing in the hearth.

The house was warm and inviting, but it looked like it had not recently benefitted from what Eamon would have termed 'a woman's touch.' The living area was dominated by a large open fire on one side and Welsh dresser on the other filled with silver trophies and medals. The bulk of the silverware seemed to be for rowing or *currach* racing, and many of them were inscribed with Marcus's name. The centrepiece was the cup Marcus won at the All-Ireland *currach*-rowing championships when he was still in his teens.

'Well, we know who to ask if we need to make a quick getaway across the sea,' O'Reilly said, admiring the trophies.

'Marcus is a spectacular oarsman who could make his boat glide effortlessly over the water, as if his body were an extension of the oars. How's the head, Sean?'

'Not too bad now, Eamon. Fidelma makes a lovely Irish coffee for breakfast, so that did the trick.'

'It usually does. It's nearly worth getting arrested just to get a mug of Fidelma's Irish coffee.'

'We're searching for this Englishman,' Dykes said, keen to wrestle the conversation back onto a professional footing. 'Do you know where he is?'

'You mean Willie. Don't worry,' Eamon said. 'I know where he is. Have some tea and we'll go and look for him when the weather dries up.'

'Are you the priest?' Dykes persisted.

Eamon laughed so hard he nearly lost control of his false teeth. 'I'm not the priest,' he explained, finally. 'But the priest will be along any minute.'

When Marcus returned home, he was not surprised to see the two garda detectives waiting for him. And neither was he surprised by the sight of his inebriated father trying to conceal the fact that he'd been drinking. Marcus had already checked the stable at the back and discovered that Eamon had liberated his secret stash of poteen.

He made a mental note to chastise his father later but, in the interim, he felt it was sufficient to just banish the old man from the kitchen, where the two officers had arranged themselves around the dining table.

He had enough on his mind without worrying about his father, and he knew it was high time he set the detectives straight about Willie.

'I know why you're looking for him and I have to say, you're barking up the wrong tree. There's no way Willie stole any money.'

'You know that for sure, do you?' Dykes asked.

'What makes you think it was him anyway? Where's your evidence?'

Dykes took out the artist's sketch and showed it to Marcus. 'Two witnesses have verified that this man paid for services at their pubs using cash that could only have come from the robbery.'

'That's Willie alright,' said Eamon. 'I'd recognise his English face anywhere.'

Marcus glared at Eamon, who put a fresh pot of tea on the table.

'That doesn't mean anything,' said Marcus. 'Hundreds of people look like that. Willie just isn't the type.

'What type is that? The type to run an illegal poteen operation with the local priest?'

Marcus averted his gaze.

'That's right, we know all about your dirty little secret. We were told by a couple in the village—' Dykes consulted his notes.

'Jimmy and Lucy,' O'Reilly said.

'—that you know everything there is to know about Willie and that you might even be in on it. Stop protecting this fella and tell us where he is.'

'Jimmy and Lucy,' Marcus exclaimed. 'Jesus Christ.'

'I don't think there's any need to take the Lord's name in vain.' Eamon poured tea in all the cups.

'So now we can assume that Jimmy and Lucy are looking for Willie because you two clowns led them to believe he stole two million euro in Galway,' Marcus shouted. 'They've probably already found him and God only knows what they're doing to him.'

'Now hang on a second—' Dykes interjected.

'It's all my fault.' Marcus held the garda sketch of the robbery suspect.

'What do you mean?' Dykes asked.

'I knew they were looking for him.' Marcus buried his head in his hands. 'And I didn't warn him.'

The priest explained everything to the detectives. He told them about Willie's illegal poteen operation, his own involvement and Lucy's desire to shut it down. Marcus explained the fight at the pub and Sarah's attempt to talk some sense into her daughter. If he had warned Willie on time, the Englishman wouldn't be missing.

'Yes, yes,' said Dykes. 'That's why they said they knew the Englishman and then tried to send me off in the wrong direction.'

'That Geraghty fella told them about the bank robbery,' said O'Reilly. 'They must have been after the stolen money.'

'That's about the size of it,' said Dykes.

Marcus wondered what Willie was doing in Galway on Tuesday night. *It couldn't be true—not Willie. The old man wouldn't have been able to rob a bank. He's nearly seventy, for God's sake.* Marcus dismissed the idea.

And then he thought about it again. Willie had been acting strange all week. He knew the Englishman had something up his sleeve, but he didn't know what. Willie wanted to sell his boat and travel the world with some mystery woman with whom he'd fallen in love. Then there was the sudden trip to Galway.

Marcus considered Jimmy and Lucy: *Willie could be in serious trouble if they think he has the money.*

'How much money are we talking about?' Eamon asked.

'One point eight million euro,' said O'Reilly.

Dykes looked at Marcus as he took a sip of his tea. 'Tell me, what's a man of the cloth doing running an illegal poteen operation and working in an illegal casino?'

Marcus smiled at the detective and looked as if he had heard the question a thousand times before. 'The parish needs money, and we have no way of raising it. I find myself doing strange things in the name of the Lord.'

'Well, it's a shame you have to resort to crime,' O'Reilly said. 'I hope you know I'll have to inform Sergeant Gilligan of your activities.'

'Fire away,' said Marcus, stifling a laugh. But he felt the rage build up inside him as he watched O'Reilly scribble the information down in his notebook.

'Settle down, Kojak,' Dykes said, laughing at his partner. 'I think we can let this one slide.'

O'Reilly was about to object when Dykes's mobile rang. Dykes answered, listened for a moment and then took out his own notebook.

'Alright, Delores, calm down. I'm on the Aran Islands now, so I can't come and see you. Can you go to the Mill Street Garda Station and find Gerry Brady, the sketch artist? Give him a description of the woman and he can fax me the sketch.'

Dykes put his hand over the mobile and turned to Marcus.

'Do you have the number of the nearest fax machine?'

'The only fax machine on the island I know about is at the clinic. The bishop uses it sometimes to contact me.'

Marcus grabbed Dykes's pen and wrote down the number while Dykes turned his attention back to the mobile. 'Alright, Delores, I'm texting you the number of the fax machine here. Ask Brady to send the sketch to that number when it's done.'

Dykes hung up the phone and turned to O'Reilly.

'Our witness at the pub in Galway remembers our suspect had a female companion. She didn't get a good look at her, but she might be able to give Brady a decent description.'

'Does your friend Willie have a girlfriend?' O'Reilly asked Marcus.

'Now that you mention it, he did say he'd met someone. But I've never seen her.'

'Maybe the sketch will jog your memory,' Dykes said. 'But now we have to find Willie. Any ideas?'

Marcus hoped Willie wasn't at home, but he knew they'd have to check there. He hoped he was off somewhere on his boat, far away from Jimmy and Lucy. With any luck, they might find the two thugs at Willie's place. 'I know where he lives and where the poteen still is located, so we can start looking there.'

Marcus rose from his seat, put on his leather jacket and kicked Judas affectionately in the rump to dislodge him from the rug at the back door. He opened the front door and let the two detectives exit first. Judas walked off at a canter and jumped onto the couch in the living room.

'If Willie turns up, tell him where we've gone,' Marcus said to Eamon.

The quickest way to get on the road to Bungowla, where they could get a boat to Rock Island, was across the beach adjacent to the farm. Marcus jumped onto the driver's seat of the jaunting car and directed his companions to sit in the back. He guided the horse through the field beside his house, down the steep hill and onto the beach.

The tide was out, so Marcus knew they'd have a clear run across the sands to the road on the other side. When he spotted Willie's boat sitting on the beach, he nearly fell off the car in surprise.

He guided the horse towards it and dreaded what he might find inside. 'Willie rarely moors his boat here. There must be something wrong.'

As they approached the yacht, Dykes and O'Reilly jumped off the jaunting car. They walked to the water's edge and braced for the cold of the sea. Dykes reached for his gun, only then remembering it had been stolen.

Soon they were all knee-deep in ice-cold water and peering in over the side of Willie's boat. O'Reilly jumped into the craft first and inspected every nook and cranny. He climbed down the small ladder to the lower cabin and looked around. Dykes and Marcus climbed aboard too. When they heard O'Reilly shout, they hurried down the steps and looked around the spacious cabin.

O'Reilly was standing ankle-deep in water and pointing at a smattering of fresh blood visible on the wall beside him. A blood-stained rope was floating in the water, along with two cigarette ends.

'This is Willie's boat?' O'Reilly waited for Marcus to nod. 'Does he smoke?'

'No, he doesn't smoke,' said Marcus. 'What does that mean?'

'It means—' O'Reilly wasn't allowed to finish his sentence.

'It means we weren't the only people looking for your friend,' Dykes continued.

The three men looked around the rest of the boat and found more evidence of a struggle.

Just as he was about to leave, Dykes spotted a dark blue baseball cap in the corner. He picked it up and showed it to O'Reilly.

'Does this remind you of anything?'

'That's the baseball cap Delores from Neo described.'

Dykes looked at it again and could see the brand name *Ford* written on it.

He placed it in his pocket and turned to Marcus.

'Your friend is in a world of trouble.'

When they'd seen enough, they made their way up the steps to the deck.

Dykes was the first to see Jimmy and Lucy standing there, waiting for them. He was also the first to see that Jimmy and Lucy were holding the detectives' garda-issue Walther P99 pistols. Both Jimmy and Lucy held out their guns and watched as the three companions came up the steps.

'Well, well…I see Laurel and Hardy are still here,' said Lucy. 'How are you enjoying your stay on our pleasant island?'

'The locals are certainly making us feel welcome,' said Dykes. 'How are tricks with you?'

'I'm at a loose end, as it happens.' Lucy looked at Jimmy and gestured for him to search the three companions for weapons.

'As you can see, we decided to confiscate your guns for safekeeping.'

'Yes, we wondered where they had got to.'

When Jimmy finished frisking the three men, he moved to the back of the boat and shepherded them off.

'We found Willie a while ago, as you'll be glad to hear, but he felt unable to divulge the whereabouts of his poteen still. I wonder if you could do the honours.'

'What have you done with him?' Marcus climbed out of the boat with the two detectives.

'Let's go back to yours for a cup of tea and discuss it, shall we?'

'I don't know what you think you know, but Willie did not steal that money in Galway,' Marcus pleaded.

'Laurel and Hardy here think otherwise, don't you, boys?'

Dykes and O'Reilly remained silent as they made their way across the beach.

'What about the horse, sweetheart?' Jimmy asked.

'The horse is fine—I think he likes the beach. Anyway, the young detective here could do with the exercise.'

Lucy held the rear as Jimmy marched the three hostages across the beach.

17

EAMON was bewildered by all the recent shenanigans and the fact that things were getting progressively more unpredictable. Leaving the mess from the tea in the kitchen, he walked into the living room. He was gagging for a drink, but he had no money—and Marcus had hidden all the poteen. Normally, the pub would be his next port of call, but he was no longer allowed any credit, thanks to his son. It was a fine state of affairs when an upstanding member of the community like him, and the father of a priest, couldn't get a drink for love or money.

He'd already resigned himself to a night of sobriety in front of the television, but then he had an idea.

Limping back into the kitchen, he grabbed two potato sacks from one of the cupboards. Tucking them under his jumper, he opened the back door and headed for the pub. If his plan worked, he'd have plenty of money for as much drink as he wanted. He couldn't do it alone, but he was sure he'd find a suitable volunteer in the pub.

When Eamon reached the back door of The Bar, he looked in through the window and saw Mattie Dwyer sitting at the counter nursing a nearly dead pint of Guinness. He opened the door and walked in.

'Soft night, Mattie,' Eamon said as he approached the counter and climbed on a stool.

'Ah good man, Eamon,' said Mattie, draining the last of his Guinness and picking up his cigarettes. 'I'm afraid I'm off now, Eamon,' he said as he climbed off his perch and headed for the door. 'No more money for drink. I'll have to be nice to the missus for tomorrow's drink.'

'I might be able to help you with that,' Eamon said as he followed Mattie out the door.

'What do you mean?'

'I'll explain as we go.'

The two men negotiated the steps down to the main road.

About twenty-five minutes later, Eamon and Mattie Dwyer dismounted their bicycles at the entrance to John Joe Stankard's yard. The lights were off and the whole place was pitch-black.

'What are you up to?' Mattie asked.

'What's that?' Eamon could barely hear his companion over the racket being made by Stankard's chickens.

'I said what are we doing here?'

'We're going to liberate a few of Stankard's chickens and sell them to the head chef abroad in the hotel.' Eamon retrieved the two sacks from under his jumper and handed one to Mattie. 'Then we'll have money for drink.'

'Hang on a minute,' said Mattie, taking the sack from Eamon. 'How did you know about Stankard's chickens?'

'What difference does it make?'

'Was it your son that told you about Stankard's chickens?'

'I suppose it was,' said Eamon, irritated. 'What difference does it make?'

'It makes plenty of difference,' said Mattie, throwing the sack to the ground. 'I see what you're up to, the pair of you. Penitent sinners go to confession and open up their hearts to your son and then he tells you how to make money out of their schemes.'

'What the fuck are you on about?' Eamon picked up the sack and handed it back to his reluctant collaborator. 'I don't know anything about penitent sinners or schemes. He mentioned to me that Stankard had a lot of chickens and that Stankard himself didn't even know how many chickens he had. So, I didn't think he would miss a few if we fecked them. How did you know it was my son that told me, anyway?'

'Never mind all that now,' said Mattie, taking the sack from Eamon. 'Let's get cracking.'

The two men dropped their bicycles on the ground and negotiated the gate at Stankard's yard.

When Mattie reached the top of the gate, a gust of wind blew his toupee clean off his head and sent it flying across the yard. The rug landed on one of the chickens and the noise level increased several octaves as the frightened birds scampered.

Just then the lights came on and the back door of Stankard's house opened.

Eamon and Mattie didn't wait to see who was coming out of the house. They jumped off the gate, grabbed their bicycles and freewheeled it down the hill toward Kilronan. Mattie manoeuvred his bicycle into Eamon's slipstream and followed effortlessly behind, his bald head gleaming in the moonlight.

Eamon didn't bother taking off his dirty boots when he entered his house. He was so disconsolate after his misadventure that he didn't notice the trail of mud he was leaving across the kitchen floor. He was just about to sit down when he heard the back door open. A gust of wind grazed his cheek and he turned around to see a giant of a man standing in the open doorway.

Jimmy Roberts approached at a nimble clip and grabbed Eamon by the arms. The old man screamed when he was pulled towards the middle of the room. Just then, Marcus and the two detectives filed into the living room, followed by Lucy.

'You're looking well, Eamon,' Lucy said with a smile.

'Let my father go,' Marcus pleaded. 'He has nothing to do with this.'

'All in good time,' said Lucy. 'Take a seat, please.'

Jimmy lined the two detectives against the wall and searched for their handcuffs. Once he found what he was looking for, he turned the detectives around so they were facing the wall. He placed the handcuffs on both Dykes and O'Reilly, then he shoved Eamon onto the sofa. Moving backwards towards the door, he closed it while keeping his gun trained on the group.

'Where does Willie live, Marcus?' Lucy said, pointed her pistol at the group.

Marcus was beginning to panic at the gravity of their situation. Apart from the general anxiety he was feeling at having a gun pointed at his head, he was concerned about Willie.

He began to realise that one of two things happened: either Jimmy had killed Willie before he'd been able to take them to his house, or the old man had escaped. The second scenario seemed less likely. Then it occurred to him that it didn't matter whether or not Willie had stolen the money. All that mattered was that Lucy thought he'd stolen it and she could have killed him for it.

'Where's Willie?' Marcus tried to hide the fear in his voice.

'He's fine,' she said. 'He just has a bit of a headache. Tell us where his house is.'

Marcus knew she was lying. If Willie was fine, Lucy wouldn't have come all the way here to ask where his house was. But Marcus had to stop worrying about Willie—there was nothing he could do about that now. He had to protect his father by figuring out a way to separate Lucy and Jimmy and somehow overpower them.

'Alright, I'll show you the house if you let us go.'

'That's my boy,' said Lucy. 'But I'm afraid we won't be letting anyone go until you show us the house.'

Lucy ordered the two youngest men, Marcus and O'Reilly, to move to one side of the room. Jimmy moved over too and kept his gun trained on them. Lucy told the other two, Eamon and Dykes, they might as well get comfortable on the sofa. She sat on the seat at the other side of the fire and continued to look menacing. The room was quiet for a minute or two, and then she stood up.

'Jimmy, make yourself useful and take the handcuffs off him,' she instructed, pointing at O'Reilly.

Jimmy walked over to the hostages and freed O'Reilly. Waving his gun at them, he ordered them to walk towards the door. Lucy kept her eyes focused on Dykes.

'Take those two to Willie's poteen still,' she said to Jimmy, 'and I'll stay with this lot.'

Jimmy nodded and pushed Marcus and O'Reilly out the door.

'Wait. Let me get my coat, will you?' said O'Reilly. It's freezing out there'.

'You better behave yourselves now,' said Lucy. 'My darling Jimmy would like nothing better than to blow your heads off.'

When the cold wind hit him full in the face, Jimmy let out an evil laugh as he pushed Marcus and O'Reilly out the door.

Lucy turned her attention to Eamon and Dykes. 'Now, my darlings, it looks like we're going to have to entertain ourselves while the boys are away. Anyone for a nice game of Russian roulette?'

The first thing Willie noticed when he regained consciousness was the biting smell of turpentine. He opened his eyes, but he couldn't see anything. The pain from several of his broken bones started to get most of his attention.

Every bone in his body seemed to ache, and he grimaced when he remembered what he had endured at the hands of Jimmy and Lucy.

He cursed himself for being weak and sending the two thugs on a wild-goose chase to his pot-still. If they bumped into Marcus or any other innocent bystanders along the way, he'd never forgive himself. Then he remembered he hadn't told them the location of his lighthouse. Before he'd been able to spill the beans, he'd fallen unconscious. But he wasn't sure if that was a good or a bad thing.

He looked up when he spotted a flash of light outside.

Willie tried to shout out when he heard a noise outside but, with his mouth taped, was unable to make a sound. He heard a scratching noise against the shed and saw more flashing lights.

'In here,' he managed to call out. 'I'm in here.'

When he heard another noise, he turned towards the door. His whimpering got louder as he saw the faint beam of a flashlight underneath the door. It opened, and a man walked in.

'Jesus Christ, is that you, Willie? Are you okay?'

Ivor rushed over to Willie and ripped the tape from his mouth.

'Good questions all, dear boy. If you would be kind enough to remove my shackles, I would be only too delighted to shed some light on my predicament.'

Ivor untied the ropes binding Willie's arms and legs.

Willie looked outside and saw a young woman standing just outside the door, holding a bottle of wine and two glasses.

'You're lucky I found you,' said Ivor. I was taking a shortcut to the village across the beach when I saw this woman. She seemed in distress, so I came down here to help.'

'A likely tale.' Willie shot Ivor a whimsical look.

Ivor lifted Willie up and allowed him to stand on his own, but Willie collapsed to the ground. Ivor reached down and picked up the Englishman. Willie looked at his rescuer, and a hint of a smile flashed across his face. Then he collapsed to the ground again.

A few minutes later, Willie had regained the use of his legs and, with the help of Ivor and his companion, managed to struggle to his boat. He explained the events of the previous twenty-four hours and emphasised the urgency of getting home.

'Are you sure you're going to be okay, Willie?'

'Never fear; I'll be right as rain in a minute or two. I'll just get some clothes out of my cabin and head over to the lighthouse. You seem to have your hands full here, anyway.'

'Just give us a buzz if you need anything.'

Willie was sure he could use some help, but he didn't want to drag Ivor or anyone else into his problems. He wasn't sure what was going on, but he decided that Jimmy and Lucy would find his home eventually, and he resolved to be ready when they did.

18

IT WAS just getting dark when Marcus and O'Reilly made their way up the hill towards Bungowla. Jimmy followed close behind with the Walther P99 concealed inside his coat as they passed a few locals on the *boreen*. He also had to occasionally remind his two hostages to act as naturally as possible. There was a hint of frost on the ground and a nasty chill off the ocean. Luckily for Jimmy, he had a hip flask full of Dunville's Three Crowns whiskey from which he took the occasional swig.

O'Reilly was furious as he struggled to keep warm. It was bad enough being taken hostage, but he cursed himself for leaving his coat back at the farm. Jimmy had hurried him out of the house so fast he'd been unable to grab it. They'd walked for ages, and he didn't think they would ever reach their destination. Now he was at the mercy of the elements and closer to death with every step. He wished he had listened to his mother and become a civil servant.

'Is there far to go?' he asked no one in particular.

'Shut the fuck up!' Jimmy shouted. 'I'll ask the questions around here.'

Jimmy had the air of a man who liked being in charge. He spent so much time getting bossed around by Lucy that it was nice being in charge now and again. Nor did he waste any time demonstrating to O'Reilly that he didn't like cops. But there was no time for fun—there was work to be done.

'Is there far to go, Marcus boy?' Jimmy shouted at the top of his voice.

'Not too far now.' Marcus had his mind on other things. He thought about Willie and wondered if the old man was safe. He was also worried about his father. Lucy was capable of anything, and her hostages could easily be dead by the time he returned.

'What did you do with Willie, Jimmy?' Marcus asked. 'Did you kill him?'

'I don't think so,' said Jimmy. 'But he didn't look too healthy when we left him.'

Marcus stopped dead in his tracks and looked at Jimmy.

'What do you mean? Did you kill him or not?'

'Did I give you permission to stop?'

'I'm not going any further until you tell me what happened to Willie.'

'Alright, stop blatherin'. Willie is fine. You'll see him soon if you do what you're told. Now get a move on.'

For a split second, Marcus allowed himself to believe that Willie was safe. He hoped the old man wasn't lying about the location of the money and that this business would all be over soon. He didn't trust Lucy, but they had a better chance of surviving if she got what she wanted.

It started raining when Brannock Island came into view. Marcus stopped, turned to Jimmy and pointed at the desolate island in the distance. 'That's it out there, beyond Brannock.'

'You must be joking,' said Jimmy. 'We can't swim out there.'

'We don't have to swim, you bloody eejit.' Marcus pointed at the *currach* behind Jimmy. 'We can use that!'

'Don't call me an eejit, ya Fenian bastard!'

When they crossed the channel and reached an inlet on the eastern side of Rock Island, Jimmy ordered his hostages out of the boat.

O'Reilly was beginning to tire, so Jimmy pointed the gun at his head and directed him onward. Jimmy knew O'Reilly was on his last legs, so he pushed the police detective across the rocky terrain and waited for him to fall over.

It didn't take long for O'Reilly to collapse, and Jimmy let out a mighty cheer when it happened. The detective struggled to his feet and cursed his tormentor with all the force he could muster. That just amused Jimmy even more, and he continued to laugh in coarse, rasping cackles. As they neared the small wooden shed at the back of the lighthouse, Jimmy quickened his pace and let the detective lag behind.

Excited by the thrill of the hunt, he could see the money already—the crisp, clean notes of red and blue. He could see them wrapped in their cosy bags, spread across the floor. But he didn't see Marcus sneak up behind him and give him a whack in the back of the head.

Marcus, though, couldn't summon up enough energy to knock Jimmy out, and O'Reilly couldn't take full advantage of the situation. Jimmy recovered just in time to raise his gun and let off several shots in the general direction of the two men.

For the first time in his short career, O'Reilly thought his life was about to end. Jimmy was pointing the gun at him, and he looked mad as hell. Just as it seemed he was going to shoot, Jimmy lowered his pistol and began laughing maniacally. That was when Marcus realised Jimmy might be under the influence of alcohol or drugs.

He watched as Jimmy shot the padlock off the door and opened it.

'You could have just used the keys,' Marcus said, holding up a set of keys.

Jimmy turned towards the two men and waved them inside. He followed O'Reilly and pushed him part of the way for good measure.

Willie's poteen shed was small but could accommodate the still and rows of shelves filled with empty bottles. It was dark and dusty, so Marcus found the light switch and turned it on.

Jimmy took a cursory look around and ordered his two hostages to sit on the floor by the wall. He took out a large roll of duct tape from inside his coat and strapped the two men together. It was an awkward job, but Jimmy managed to complete it. When he was sure they were secure, he rose to his feet and looked around.

Now that he had all the loose ends tied up, Jimmy did what he'd been dying to do all day. He walked over to the poteen still and looked underneath. He showed no annoyance when he failed to find the money the first time, but he became furious later after he ripped the apparatus apart and still came up empty-handed. Jimmy was a trusting man by nature, so he was angry that Willie had lied to him, especially since he'd given the old man every incentive to tell the truth.

He was so angry, in fact, that he tore the whole shed apart. He pulled down the walls plank by plank and then all the wooden joists. He knocked over the still and made sure there were no secret hiding places he had overlooked. There was soon nothing left of the shed. The three men found themselves in the open air, surrounded by loose lumber and broken bottles.

Jimmy took off his coat and started rummaging through the pockets. He took out a small bag of marijuana from the inside pocket and rested the coat on the ground. Mumbling to himself, he opened the bag, picked up a pack of Rizla and removed a rolling paper. He grabbed a portion of the weed, spread it evenly on the paper and rolled it into a compact joint. Putting it in his mouth, he lit it and took a long, satisfying drag.

Glaring at his two hostages with menace in his eyes, he laughed. 'Fenian bastards.'

Marcus was confident Jimmy had become too inebriated to maintain his composure. Even though O'Reilly had fallen unconscious, Marcus believed he could neutralise Jimmy and get back to the house to tackle Lucy. He could feel a shard of glass with his fingertips, and he tried to manoeuvre it closer to the duct tape on his wrists. When the edge of the glass was touching the tape, he moved his fingers up and down in a sliding motion.

After some time, he could feel his bindings giving way.

He had visited Rock Island many times in the past and knew they were sitting just a few hundred metres from a sheer cliff. Considering his options, he decided the only way to overpower Jimmy would be to lure him to the cliff edge and somehow trick him into falling over the side. The moral implications of his plan were not lost on him, but he hoped Jimmy would have a quick death without too much pain. Considering all the people Jimmy had harmed and was continuing to hurt, Marcus thought it would be churlish not to put an end to the thug's reign of terror. It was for the greater good, he told himself.

'What's the difference between an apple and an orange?' Marcus asked Jimmy.

'What?' Jimmy took a swig out of his hip flask.

'There's no such thing as an apple bastard.'

Jimmy thought about it for a moment, and then a flash of rage spread across his face. He leapt from his seat and lunged at Marcus. The priest managed to free himself from the duct tape in the nick of time. He shifted to the side and watched as Jimmy hurtled past him, grasping at thin air as he fell on the limestone ground.

Marcus snapped Jimmy up by the hair and dragged him a few metres across the stone. He could remember losing his temper only a few times before—but it was never like this. He had once thrown a bucket of milk at the door of the horse shed when one of the cows stepped on his foot during milking. But he could never imagine losing his temper at another human being and causing pain in a fit of rage.

And yet here he was, dragging another man across the ground with the intention of killing him. There were no two ways about it—Marcus wanted to kill Jimmy and nothing was going to stop him. It would take weeks in confession to make up for it—he would probably give poor old Flaherty a heart attack in the process. Rather than mull the theological ramifications of his actions, he tried to concentrate on the matter at hand.

Jimmy writhed and wriggled in a desperate effort to break free. When he managed to loosen Marcus's grip, he rolled around on the ground in an attempt to face his opponent. He kicked out to prevent the priest from attacking and managed to raise himself off the ground, but Marcus still had the advantage of higher ground. Jimmy lunged again for Marcus, and again the priest managed to step out of the way in time. Jimmy fell, but he was able to pick up a rock in the process. He turned, aimed and threw the stone in Marcus's direction.

Marcus's vision was hampered by the darkness and he didn't see the rock until it was too late. The stone grazed his ear—it barely made contact, but it was enough to cause considerable pain. Marcus fell back slightly and Jimmy leapt forward, catching Marcus right in the chest and causing both of them to fall to the rocky ground. Marcus took a firm hold of the lapels of Jimmy's jacket as the effects of drink and drugs started to take their toll on his foe. They wriggled around for a while with neither man able to gain the upper hand. Marcus kept a tight grip of the Northerner and considered how to bring the drama to a close.

It was clear to Marcus that Jimmy was stronger than he was, but Marcus was the fitter, thanks to the hours he spent rowing every day. He was proud of himself for not only matching Jimmy punch for punch but also going the distance. It wasn't every day a parish priest found it necessary to beat people up but when it was required, he was glad he was up to the task.

The momentary silence was broken by the sound of 'Ave Maria' emanating from inside Marcus's jacket. Marcus felt his phone vibrating in his pocket and knew his worst fears were realised. 'I'll have to get that,' he said, 'it might be important.'

'Fire away,' said Jimmy, 'I'm going nowhere.'

They both stood up and eyed each other suspiciously. Marcus pushed Jimmy away and, when there was sufficient distance between them, he reached his left hand into his pocket and took out the phone. He raised it to his face and frowned when he saw who was calling.

'What is it, Margaret?' he said. 'I'm a bit tied up at the moment.'

'I was just calling to say I won't be in tomorrow,' Margaret bellowed on the other end of the line. 'I have a hair appointment in Galway.'

'That's fair enough,' Marcus said. 'Have a nice time.'

He switched off the phone and threw it on the grass beside them.

'Margaret has a hair appointment in Galway tomorrow,' Marcus said to Jimmy.

'That's good to know.' Jimmy ran towards Marcus with his head down.

Marcus raised his right leg and kicked Jimmy in the stomach kung-fu style. He inched his way backwards toward the edge of the cliff, making sure to keep his eye on Jimmy.

'There's nowhere to hide,' Jimmy shouted as Marcus got even closer to the edge.

Marcus gambled on the fact that Jimmy didn't know how near they were to the abyss. He hoped the big man was stupid enough to take a run at him.

Sure enough, Jimmy darted forward like a rampaging bull. Marcus smiled as Jimmy got closer, picking up speed as he went. He watched as Jimmy ran, getting forever closer to his doom. He could just about hear the crashing waves in the darkness and Jimmy was a mere hair's breadth away. Marcus dropped to the ground and remained motionless as Jimmy tripped over his kneeling body and careened over the cliff.

'Fenian bastard!' was all Marcus could hear, with the words trailing off as Jimmy fell.

Marcus stood up and took his holy stole out of his pocket. He faced the cliff, kneeled and placed the stole around his neck. He performed the Last Rites for the dearly departed, even though he knew Jimmy didn't deserve it.

When he got back to where the shed used to be, Marcus picked up Jimmy's coat and extricated the gun and the whiskey flask from the pockets. Placing the gun in his pocket, he walked over to O'Reilly, who was still unconscious. He slapped him in the face a couple of times and watched as the detective open his eyes. Marcus took out the flask and opened it. 'Drink some of this.'

O'Reilly had a nasty gash above his right eye, but he'd survive. He looked all around and rested his eyes on Marcus.

'Where's Jimmy? What happened?'

'I'll tell you later.' Marcus went around to O'Reilly's back and started unravelling the duct tape. 'Do you feel like walking back to my place?'

'Gimme another drop of that whiskey and I'll be fine.'

Marcus undid the bindings and handed O'Reilly the whiskey flask.

'I suppose that's the end of Jimmy,' said O'Reilly.

'I suppose it is.'

O'Reilly stood and felt dizzy for a moment. He walked over to the lighthouse and went in through the open door. Looking around, he spotted one of Willie's overcoats and borrowed it for the walk back to Cockle Strand.

Marcus and O'Reilly made good time as they walked along silently and considered their lucky escape. It could have ended differently if Marcus hadn't found the shard of glass to cut the duct tape. But there was still a lot of work to be done and hostages to be liberated. After a while, neither man could feel the cold as they concentrated on the task at hand.

When they reached the sandy stretch of beach near the Nees' farm, they stopped briefly and formulated a plan to overpower Lucy. They had the element of surprise, which was never to be underestimated.

'At least you have the training for this sort of thing,' Marcus said. 'I'm just a poor priest.'

'I don't know; you were fairly handy back there!'

Marcus took the handgun out of his pocket and made a show of bracing the weapon using both hands. He handed it to O'Reilly.

'I nearly forgot about this. Yours, I believe.'

O'Reilly smiled as he took the gun and checked that it was loaded.

'Do you think Lucy will be angry about Jimmy?' Marcus joked as the two men made their way up the hill towards the farm.

'Quite furious, I think, dear boy,' came a familiar voice from the top of the hill.

Marcus could hardly believe his eyes when Willie appeared from behind a clump of bushes. The Englishman reached out to hug his friend, who began to ask a steady stream of questions.

'No time for that now, old dear,' Willie said. 'The battle beckons.'

Marcus and O'Reilly inspected Willie and found he was worse for wear. His nose was clearly broken, as was the index finger on his left hand. The entire left side of his face was swollen. He also had two black eyes and could barely see out of either.

O'Reilly had plenty of questions for Willie, but he decided this was not the time.

'You better stay here,' the detective said in as considerate a tone as he could muster. 'We'll come back for you later and bring you to a hospital.'

'I don't know who you are, sir, but you had better keep your condescending remarks to yourself.'

Marcus was about to object when Willie raised his hands.

'Now look here, I did my fair share of brawling in the sixties. We may only have been hippies, but I did my bit.'

Marcus smiled and decided Willie was up to the challenge.

The three men walked on towards the farm and braced for action.

19

SARAH Shannon didn't know for sure why she was walking towards the Nees' farm. All she knew was that her daughter was on the warpath and she had to do something to help Marcus and Willie. There was no point just sitting at home and waiting for the inevitable phone call telling her that one of them had been hurt. Her daughter's well-being was also a priority. Lucy loved her, even though she had been nothing but trouble since she was born. There was no doubt Lucy would end up in jail again sooner or later, but that was alright by Sarah as long as she didn't get hurt.

Sarah walked down the hill to the Nees' house but she didn't know what she would do when she got there. The least she could do was keep Marcus company, and help him if Lucy turned up. In the distance, Sarah could see that the lights were on. She could also feel a sense of dread in the pit of her stomach as she got closer. It didn't seem fair to her that Lucy's problems were taking front and centre just when she was starting to make sense of her own dysfunctional life. Just when she had escaped an abusive relationship with her most recent boyfriend and had come to terms with her feelings towards Marcus, her world had started falling apart again. Lucy was messing everything up with her self-indulgent temper tantrums.

If Lucy hadn't been armed and dangerous, she would have disciplined her the old-fashioned way. Sarah had decided she had to get out of Ireland for a while, no matter what the outcome of Lucy's misadventures. She needed to put some distance between her and all the things in her life that were causing her distress.

When her boyfriend had been sentenced to a lengthy jail term for assaulting a garda detective, Sarah started to get her own life back on track. She'd set up a good life for herself in Galway, but the Aran Islands kept pulling her back. Having secured a job as a pharmacist, she found an apartment and leased a reliable Nissan Micra. Everything had been going well until she received a call from one of her old school friends informing her that Lucy had been up to her old tricks. She knew Marcus wanted to deal with the situation himself, but Sarah had come over to the island anyway, out of a sense of duty.

As Sarah approached the farmhouse, she was surprised to see the front door wide open. It was strange for them to leave it open on such a cold night. She walked up to the side window to get an idea of what was going on inside.

She cursed under her breath when she saw her daughter pointing a gun at two other people in the room. She recognised Eamon, but she didn't know the other man. She couldn't see Marcus or Willie anywhere and hoped Lucy hadn't killed anyone.

Sarah walked around the house to get the lay of the land. Marcus might be lying unconscious somewhere, or Jimmy might be lurking. She made her way to the rear, careful not to trip over any farm equipment or disturb the livestock.

When she got to the back door, she could see that it, too, was wide open. She passed by silently and carried on walking around the house.

When she arrived back at the front door, she was satisfied there were no surprises waiting, but she still couldn't figure out how to confront Lucy. It wouldn't do to go in all guns blazing because she had no guns—anyway, the last thing she wanted was for someone to get hurt. She decided to go with the softly-softly approach.

Peering into the house through the open door, she called out Lucy's name.

'Who the fuck is that?' said Lucy.

'It's me—your mother.' Sarah entered through the open door. 'Put the gun down, like a good girl.'

'Stay where you are,' Lucy ordered. 'I don't take orders from you anymore.'

Lucy got up from her chair and backed away to the far end of the living room. She pointed the gun at her mother and gestured for her to join the two men on the sofa.

'Go on,' Lucy shouted. 'Sit on the sofa.'

Sarah waited for a moment and then did as she was told. Dykes and Eamon shuffled to the left to make room.

'You're not going to get away with this,' Dykes vowed. 'My colleagues will be here when they realise I haven't checked in.'

'That doesn't concern me.' Lucy had resumed her position on the armchair. 'We'll be away with the money by the time your friends arrive.'

'Where will you go?' Sarah asked.

'What do you care? You never gave a shit about me before.'

'I have always loved you, Lucy. It wasn't easy on my own, you know.'

'You had Father Trendy to help you, didn't you? He was always ready with my suitcase whenever I got in the way.'

'It wasn't like that.' Sarah tried to turn her head to look at Lucy. 'We were only trying to do what was best for you.'

'You thought six years in a convent and another six months in prison was the best for me?'

'Don't do this, Lucy. You're causing a lot of trouble for a lot of people.'

'Why are you here, Mother dearest? Why aren't you off shaggin' that fuckin' priest?'

'Don't talk to me like that, you ungrateful bitch.' Sarah rose from the sofa in a fit of anger. 'How dare you? Marcus and I are friends, that's all. Why do you always have to think the worst of everybody?'

Lucy struggled to regain control of the situation in the wake of her mother's outburst. She regained her composure and trained the gun back on Sarah.

'Sit down, Mother.'

Sarah sat back down but was unable to stop the flood of tears. Eamon reached over and tried to place a comforting hand on Sarah's knee.

'Keep your hands to yourself, you dirty old fucker,' Lucy barked, keeping the gun trained on the three of them.

'I was just trying to help,' Eamon pleaded. 'Can't you see she's upset?'

'It's alright, Eamon,' Sarah wept. 'She doesn't care about anyone but herself.'

'How are you going to get off the island once you have the money?' Dykes asked.

'Never you mind—we have a plan.'

'No, you don't. You have no idea what sort of trouble you're in, and there's no way out of it. The whole island will be surrounded by cops by morning, and they'll have helicopters, gunboats, you name it.'

'Are you taking the piss?' Lucy walked over to Dykes and trained the gun on him. 'There will be half a dozen cops at the most, and all they'll have at their disposal will be a few donkeys and truncheons. I think we can deal with that.'

'You're wrong—I called my superiors in Galway while we were inspecting the yacht and I told them all about you. They know your names and descriptions and they'll be coming in with guns blazing because I confirmed you were armed and dangerous. Have you ever seen *Butch Cassidy and the Sundance Kid*? Well, that's how you're going to end up.'

Eamon looked at Dykes with a worried expression on his face. 'I don't remember Butch and Sundance having hostages.'

'What the fuck are you two on about? Butch and who?'

'They were—'

'Never mind that, just stay quiet.' Lucy got up from the chair and started pacing the room.

'You could just end this now and let us go,' Sarah pleaded. 'Sergeant Dykes is handcuffed, so he can't stop you. I'll go with you and help you get back to the mainland.'

'I'm going to wait for the money.' Lucy scratched her head. 'I mean, I'm going to wait for Jimmy and the money.'

20

MARCUS peered through the side window and saw that Lucy was still standing in the living room, pointing her gun at the hostages. O'Reilly was also monitoring the situation over Marcus's shoulder.

The priest nearly fell back with shock when he saw Sarah sitting on the sofa next to Eamon and Dykes. He consoled himself with the fact that the hostages seemed to be sitting comfortably. Except for the fact that Lucy was holding a gun, it looked for all the world like a normal family enjoying a quiet night at home. It almost seemed like a shame to disturb them.

They stayed outside for a while and waited for Willie to carry out the prearranged diversion. The old man was supposed to make noises at the back of the farmhouse to distract Lucy while Marcus and O'Reilly barged in through the front door.

Marcus was reluctant to allow Willie to take the responsibility, but the Englishman insisted on doing his part.

O'Reilly cursed the fact that they had only one gun and that Marcus had made him give it to Willie. The Englishman claimed he knew how to use it. The detective leaned against a barrel by the side of the house and cursed as it fell over. Luckily, it landed on the grass and made no noise. He looked in the window again to make sure Lucy had heard nothing.

Seconds later, they heard loud banging noises coming from the rear of the house. Marcus looked at Judas. 'Stay here or I'll kill you myself.'

Marcus edged his way towards the front door. He waited for a signal from O'Reilly, who was still watching through the window. Marcus eased the door open.

Eamon looked up when he saw Marcus. He elbowed Sarah in the ribs and gestured towards him. Lucy was looking through the kitchen window and didn't see Marcus sneak up behind her. He made it all the way across the floor before she turned around. When she realised what was happening, he'd tackled her and wrestled her to the floor.

Lucy was pinned under Marcus, but she kept hold of the gun. She managed to shoot at O'Reilly, who was running towards her with outstretched arms. The first shot missed him but the second hit him in the right lung. He tripped over Judas, who had darted between his legs, and fell to the floor next to Marcus.

Lucy wriggled out from under Marcus and stood up. She bounded across the room and grabbed Eamon by the hair, pulling him off the sofa. Moving along the wall towards the door, she used Eamon as a shield. Marcus and Dykes were powerless to act as Lucy waved the pistol in the air, shouting obscenities across the room. Judas started barking as the shouting grew louder.

'I'll kill him, do you hear? I'll kill him!' she shouted.

'There's no way out of this, Lucy,' Dykes said. 'Just put the gun down.'

'Where's Jimmy? What have you done to Jimmy?'

'Jimmy's alright,' Willie lied as he entered the room. 'We overpowered him and tied him up. If you put the gun down, you can go and see him.'

'You're a lying bastard.'

Lucy moved closer to the front door.

'He's up in Kilmurvey, old girl,' Willie pleaded, 'tied to a gate beside John Joe Stankard's top field. You can't miss him.'

Willie didn't know what Lucy would find at the gate beside Stankard's field, but at least she'd be far away.

'But sure he'll be pecked to death by Stankard's chickens by the time you get to him,' Eamon said. 'He has a hundred of the bastards.' Everyone except Lucy shot Eamon a disapproving glance.

'He doesn't have as many as you might think,' Marcus corrected him.

'Come on, Lucy. Go and find Jimmy and leave us be.' Sarah rose from the sofa, but Lucy gestured for her to stay where she was. 'Let us take that detective to the clinic. You'll be in worse trouble if he dies.'

Lucy kept her eyes on her mother. She wasn't paying attention when Marcus looked behind him and gestured to Willie to hand him his gun. Marcus raised the gun and looked his father in the eye. 'I'm sorry about this, Pop.'

'Wait a minute.' Eamon realised his son was aiming the gun at him. 'Remember the Fourth Commandment: honour thy father!'

'I'm sorry—it's the only way.'

'You've never shot a gun in your life, you bloody eejit.'

'Shut the fuck up, the lot of you,' Lucy advised. 'I'll kill him, Marcus. I swear to God I'll kill him.'

'God doesn't listen to you anymore,' Willie said.

Marcus squeezed the trigger and nearly fell over when the gun went off. The bullet hit Eamon's prosthetic limb and knocked it clean off. Lucy couldn't hold on to Eamon and was left unprotected when the old man fell to the ground. She fired a shot into the air, causing everyone to close their eyes.

When Marcus looked up, she was gone.

He ran over to where his father was lying and kneeled beside him.

'Are you alright?'

'I'm fine, no thanks to you.'

'I had to do it. I knew she'd never be able to hold your dead weight once you fell.'

'I'd like to hear you explain that to the bishop at your next confession.'

'This doesn't look good,' said Dykes, who managed to get up off the sofa to inspect his partner. 'We'll have to get him some medical attention.'

When he straightened up, Dykes found himself face to face with Willie.

'Oh, it's you, old chap? What the devil are you doing here?'

Dykes was startled for a moment as Sarah rushed over to tend to Eamon. He stared at the Englishman and didn't see that O'Reilly was staring at him in wide-eyed disbelief.

'What's going on here, sergeant?' O'Reilly was still on the floor, writhing in agony. 'Do you know this man?'

'It would appear so,' Dykes said. 'He's the man I'm buying the boat from.'

'How do you know this lad?' Marcus walked over to Willie.

'It all seems a bit far-fetched, dear boy,' Willie stammered. 'It's been an eventful night.'

'Where did you hide the money?' O'Reilly shouted at Willie.

Willie ignored the question and walked over to a vacant chair by the fire. In the last twenty-four hours he had been beaten, tortured and imprisoned; now he just wanted to rest.

'You were in Galway recently, weren't you?' O'Reilly refused to be ignored.

The young detective knew there was something strange going on, and he wanted to get to the bottom of it. He was a police detective, after all, and this old man was the prime suspect in a criminal inquiry. Dykes recognised Willie, that was obvious, and he wanted to know why. He also wanted to know where Willie had hidden the purloined money. O'Reilly couldn't let these questions go unanswered, even if he was badly injured.

'You stole the money when you went to Galway!' the detective tried again.

'Hang on a minute.' Marcus sat next to his friend. 'Let me talk to him.'

'I went to Galway to sell my boat. I moored her at the docks so this fellow could view her,' Willie said, pointing at Dykes.

'What about the money?' Marcus prodded. 'They say you have money from a robbery.'

'Why does everyone think I stole the bloody money just because I was in Galway at the same time as the robbery?'

'Because you've been spending stolen cash all over the place,' said Dykes. 'Witnesses have described you to a tee.'

'I was only spending the money you gave me for the boat. I just—' Willie pointed at Dykes. 'It was you. You stole the money.'

Everyone turned around to look at Dykes, who backed away towards the far wall.

'Why didn't you say anything when you saw the boat today on the beach?' O'Reilly was still on the ground, listening to everything. 'You've been dragging your heels on the investigation, and now I know why. I couldn't make heads nor tails of it at first, but now it makes perfect sense.'

'I couldn't be sure it was the same boat. When I first saw her it was dark and the boat wasn't flooded.'

'You stole the money, didn't you?' O'Reilly raised his head just enough to look at Dykes.

Before Dykes could deny the accusation, O'Reilly began to laugh.

'You came across the money on Shop Street, and you decided to keep it. The pieces of the puzzle are beginning to take shape. But then you had to cover your tracks, didn't you? Send the police in the wrong direction? You remembered your meeting with Willie. You thought Willie lived in England, so you gave him some of the money as a deposit on the boat. You thought Willie would go back to England and lodge the cash in a bank. But you were wrong, weren't you? Willie didn't live in England—he lived here!'

O'Reilly tried to lift his head further, but the pain was too much.

'When you were told the cash had turned up in the Aran Islands, you had to make sure you were in charge of the investigation. You sent us around in circles so we would never find Willie.'

Dykes couldn't take anymore. He was sick of all these groundless accusations.

'It's clear we're getting nowhere. I am the senior detective, and I consider everyone here to be persons of interest in this investigation. We will all stick together until this gets sorted out.'

'In the meantime, Lucy is on the run,' Marcus pointed out. 'She's got a gun and there's no telling what she'll do when she comes up empty-handed at Stankard's field.'

'Would you mind going after her?' Dykes turned to show Marcus his handcuffed hands. 'I'm still a bit tied up. You have a fair idea where she's headed, right?'

Marcus nodded and looked at O'Reilly, who was losing a lot of blood and seemed to be drifting in and out of consciousness.

'Okay, you lot get to the clinic, and I'll go after Lucy.'

He turned to leave but Sarah grabbed him by the arm. 'Not without me.'

'I don't think that's a good idea,' Willie piped up.

'He's right,' said Marcus.

'She's my daughter. I'm the only one who can talk any sense into her.' Sarah grabbed her coat and was out the door before Marcus could object.

Marcus looked at Judas. 'Stay here, you strange dog.'

21

THE centre of Kilronan village was usually as quiet as a tomb at that time of night. Mattie Dwyer's bicycle rental shop was normally closed, and Mattie himself was generally drunk as a lord at The Bar. However, none of those things appeared to be the case when Marcus and Sarah, followed by Judas, turned the corner at the Tweed Shop and watched the drama unfolding before them.

Half the village, it seemed, was standing outside the bike shop watching events take their course. The other half was enjoying the spectacle from the beer garden at The Bar, which had laid out extra tables and chairs for the occasion.

Marcus could see straight away that the bicycle shop had been broken into. The pane of glass on the door was broken and the door was wide open. Several bikes were strewn across the street and Mattie was gesticulating wildly while talking to Sergeant Gilligan.

'What's all the commotion?' Marcus shouted at Margaret Sheridan.

Margaret broke off her heated discussion with Fidelma and allowed a sneer of disapproval to creep across her face at the sight of the priest and his companion.

'Her criminal of a daughter is after breakin' into poor old Mattie's shop,' Margaret explained, pointing at Sarah, 'and tearin' away up the hill with one of his bicycles.'

'Settle down, Margaret.' Marcus made his way through the crowd and managed to attract the attention of Sergeant Gilligan.

'I know where she's gone, Seamus.' Marcus grabbed one of the bicycles and handed it to Sarah, who had also managed to make her way through the crowd. 'You stay here and we'll go and get her.'

'That won't be necessary, Father. I was about to give chase myself. I am the garda officer, after all. I was just getting a description of the bicycle.'

'You don't understand, Seamus. She has a gun.'

'All the more reason for you not to get involved. I am trained for this sort of thing.'

'It's been thirty years since you were trained.' Marcus took the Walther P99 out of his pocket and showed it to Gilligan. 'Besides, I have a gun and you don't.'

With that, the crowd dispersed in a flurry of shouts and screams. Gilligan watched as Marcus picked up a bicycle and jumped onto it.

'Ah well…in that case, you better go. I'll just stay here and take a few more statements.'

'You do that.'

Marcus started pedalling and followed Sarah out of the square. He frowned when he spotted Judas following close behind. He was forced to stop when they got out of the village because it was too dark for them to see the road ahead. He fiddled with the dynamo on the back wheel and started pedalling again, happy to discover that the light at the front was working.

'You better keep your light off in case Lucy is lying in wait,' Marcus said to Sarah. 'I'll turn off my light when we get to Kilmurvey.'

'What are you going to do with her when you catch her?'

'I don't know. I just want to get that bloody gun off her so she doesn't shoot anyone.'

Marcus elected to avoid the shorter route through Oghil in favour of the longer coast road. The lengthier route had fewer hills and they were less likely to bump into Lucy, who would undoubtedly have chosen the quicker route. He knew Lucy would reach Stankard's gate before them, but he hoped she'd hang around long enough for them to confront her.

As they neared the hamlet of Kilmurvey, Marcus wished he were wearing gloves to protect his hands against the wind coming in from Galway Bay. He held out his hand to alert Sarah and then brought his bicycle to an abrupt stop. Placing his bike against the stone wall, he rubbed his hands together to warm them.

'We better go through the fields from here on out. It's not far to the gate, so let's hope she has a torch or something.'

Marcus helped Sarah as she climbed the stone wall bordering the pasture, then negotiated the wall himself and landed on the other side. Stankard's field was next to the one they were in, he reckoned, so they only needed to climb one more wall. He looked up at the sky and knew the overcast conditions would negate any advantage the nearly full moon might have given them.

Negotiating the fields of Inis Mór was not an easy task, especially at night. They weren't covered in lush, green grass like most farm acreage in Ireland—they were typically full of boulders and smaller rocks that provided a worthy impediment for even the most athletic trespassers.

Marcus turned around when he heard a sloshing sound behind him. Sarah had walked onto some soft mud and her boot got left behind in the slush when she'd lifted her leg. She stayed motionless as Marcus retrieved the boot and placed it back on her foot.

'Thanks. Those are my favourite socks.'

'Did I get you those for Christmas?'

'You did in your bollocks—Lucy gave me those when she was eight or nine.'

When they reached the end of the field, Marcus peered over the wall into Stankard's property to see if Lucy was at the gate. The coast seemed to be clear, so he gestured for Sarah to climb over. He helped her up and then followed.

Marcus landed on a small rock and let out an audible growl when he hit the ground. He was sure he'd twisted his ankle. Seeing some movement by the gate, which was only about fifty metres away, he gestured for Sarah to lie low.

Just then, two shots rang out in the night sky. Marcus could see the flash of light from the gun discharge, and he knew the shots came from the general direction of the gate.

'Stop shooting, Lucy. It's me—your mother!'

'Who else is with you?'

'It's just me. I'm on my own.'

'Why are you sneaking around in the field?'

'I had a puncture, and then I got lost.'

Marcus crawled between the rocks and tried to get closer to the gate without being seen.

'Keep her talking,' he whispered.

'Were they lying about Jimmy? Is he dead?'

'I don't know. Why don't you put the gun down and we'll talk?'

Sarah peered out over one of the rocks, but she couldn't see Marcus. Just then, Lucy stepped onto the middle rung of the gate and fired a shot into the field.

Marcus let out a painful shriek and then remained silent for some time.

'Marcus, are you okay?' Sarah shouted.

'Not really. She shot me in the shoulder.'

'I thought you said you were alone,' Lucy shouted at her mother.

'I'm going over there to see if he's alright. Don't shoot, okay?'

'I didn't know it was Marcus,' Lucy pleaded. 'I was just trying to frighten you.'

Lucy dropped her gun and opened the gate. She walked over to where Marcus was lying and arrived at the same time as her mother.

'I'm sorry, Mum. I just got excited. Is he still alive?'

Sarah knelt beside Marcus and inspected his wound.

'It looks like you hit him in the shoulder. You'll have to head over to Stankard's and borrow his motorbike. He's losing blood, but he'll be okay if we get him to the clinic.'

Lucy kneeled on the other side of Marcus.

'Why did you have to sneak up on me like that?' she said to him. 'I could have killed you.'

'I thought that was the idea,' Marcus said.

'I never wanted to kill anyone.' Lucy used her jacket to stem the flow of blood from Marcus's shoulder. 'We only stole the guards' guns to stop them using them on us. We never meant to shoot anyone.'

'You better hurry with that bloody motorbike,' Sarah said.

'Right, I'll be back in a minute. Keep pressure on the wound.'

'Since when do you know anything about medicine?'

'I dunno—I heard it in a movie.'

Lucy walked away as Judas appeared out of nowhere and began licking Marcus's face.

SATURDAY

22

ABHISHEK Gupta was the only doctor on call when Dykes and Eamon brought O'Reilly and Willie into the Inis Mór Clinic. In fact, he was the only doctor on the island. The clinic had plenty of nurses, but only one of them was on duty. Rosalie O'Grady took one look at O'Reilly and got on the phone to alert the other three nurses to get in as quickly as possible. The main section of the clinic had three beds and was usually only used for emergencies. In the back was a small, sterilised operating room where minor surgery was carried out.

When O'Reilly and Willie were placed on their respective beds, Dykes and Eamon had nothing to do but wait.

'What part of Ireland are you from?' Eamon asked Gupta as the doctor checked Willie's injuries.

'I'm from Calcutta,' Gupta said. 'And before you ask, I am a proper doctor.'

'Are there no Irish doctors anymore?'

Gupta ignored the comment and focused his attention on O'Reilly. He pulled the curtain around the detective's bed and got to work.

When he had graduated from the University College of Medical Sciences in Calcutta five years before, Doctor Gupta had never imagined that he would end up being the only physician on a remote Irish island. He failed to secure a position at a British hospital and was forced to apply at the Health Service Executive, which got him a job at University Hospital Galway. He'd spent a few years there before being sent to Inis Mór. So far, the most demanding medical procedure he'd performed had been lancing a boil.

He could see that the main threats to O'Reilly's life were blood loss and a collapsed lung. The first thing he did was insert a plastic tube through the skin between the ribs and into the chest cavity. O'Reilly had lost more than half the blood in his body and couldn't afford to lose anymore.

Gupta could see a clean slit-shaped bullet hole, slightly wider than a centimetre, below O'Reilly's left armpit. No exit hole was visible, so he assumed the bullet was still inside.

The duty nurse took O'Reilly's blood pressure. His pulse was rapid, he looked pale and he was clammy. When the other nurses arrived, they inserted IV lines in both arms and started infusing fluid. They also placed an arterial line in the left wrist and a catheter in the bladder.

Nurse O'Grady listened with a stethoscope to O'Reilly's chest.

'The breathing is fainter on the left side, doctor,' she said.

'Okay, that means the left lung has collapsed.'

They gave O'Reilly oxygen through a plastic tube below his nostrils. With the IV lines in place, the blood transfusion began. The clinic didn't have a lot of blood on hand, but Gupta hoped it would be enough. He was thankful that Marcus had organised a blood drive only the week before.

A nurse administered oxygen by face mask, but O'Reilly was still having trouble breathing and continued coughing up blood. His breathing was fast and laboured. His blood pressure started rising and he looked pale and grey. Beneath the oxygen mask, his lips were caked with dried blood.

'His blood pressure is not encouraging,' one of the nurses shouted.

'He has a lot of blood in his chest,' said the doctor. 'We'll have to perform surgery to stop the blood loss.'

Dykes and Eamon watched as O'Reilly was wheeled out to the back room, followed by nurses carrying all manner of equipment. Only one nurse stayed behind to treat Willie. Gupta approached the two men and couldn't conceal the worried look on his face.

'After entering his body,' he told them, 'the bullet ricocheted off the seventh rib on his left side. It's lodged about three centimetres from the heart, and it caused the lung to collapse.'

'Will he make it, doctor?' Dykes asked.

'We'll know more when we go in and take a look. Please make yourselves comfortable and be patient.'

The doctor disinfected his hands and then entered the sterilised theatre.

Hours after O'Reilly's operation, Dykes sat by his partner's side and willed him to regain consciousness. He couldn't hide the relief on his face when the young officer finally opened his eyes.

O'Reilly stared at the medal on his partner's keyring and smiled.

'Are you going to tell me what you won it for?' O'Reilly asked.

'I haven't decided.'

'Ah, go on,' said O'Reilly, you know you want to.'

Dykes stared up at the ceiling as if he expected one of the light fixtures to fall and strike him down. 'Conspicuous bravery,' he mumbled.

'What?'

'That's what I won the Scot Medal for. Conspicuous bravery in the face of overwhelming danger.'

The machines connected to O'Reilly started beeping as the young officer closed his eyes. Dykes leaned over and grabbed O'Reilly by the shoulder.

'Stay with me, son,' Dykes said. 'It happened in Dublin when I was with the Garda Emergency Response Unit. Seven civilians were being held hostage in a bank by the IRA. I was young and stupid. I went in during the shootout and led them to safety.'

'That was brave of you,' O'Reilly said, opening his eyes.

'Not really. I was still drunk from the night before, so I wasn't thinking clearly. The gunfire was giving me a headache and I just wanted it to end. I wouldn't have done it if I was sober.'

O'Reilly smiled at his partner.

Dykes and Eamon turned their heads when the doors swung open. They watched as Lucy and Sarah barged into the clinic carrying Marcus on an old door they'd found in a field. Two nurses raced over to them with a gurney, a drip unit and various other paraphernalia.

'One gunshot to the shoulder,' Sarah shouted with the air and confidence of a seasoned medic. 'He's lost a lot of blood.'

'You've been getting in a bit of shooting practice, Lucy?' Dykes quipped.

'It wasn't my fault,' Lucy pleaded. 'It was an accident.'

Gupta dropped the charts he was writing on and rushed over to examine Marcus as the nurses wheeled him into the emergency unit. They parked the gurney beside the last remaining bed and grabbed hold of the patient, carefully transferring him onto the bed.

'Is anyone here a blood relative?' the doctor asked the assembled crowd.

Dykes, Sarah and Lucy all looked at Eamon, who raised his hand. 'I'm his father.'

'Wait a minute, you can't take his blood,' Sarah shouted. 'No offence, Eamon, but there's more alcohol than blood in your body.'

'Where do you suggest we get the blood?' Gupta asked.

Sarah turned to her daughter. 'Lucy, you have O negative blood, the same as Marcus. Will you donate your blood?'

Lucy nodded her head. Gupta gestured for one of the nurses to take Lucy to another room to test the blood and start the blood transfusion. A nurse began removing Marcus's clothes while another started cleaning the wound.

'Is this necessary?' Marcus asked. 'It's just a flesh wound.'

Nobody seemed to be listening to him. A nurse swung the curtain around the bed as Gupta pulled on a fresh pair of surgical gloves. Marcus was soon connected to nearly every machine in the room by the time a nurse returned with a large bag of Lucy's blood.

'This will knock you out for a bit while I go in and take out the bullet.' Gupta injected Marcus with a needle. 'I need you to count backwards from ten.'

'Ten, nine, eight—' and then Marcus was out like a light.

Once the bullet was removed, the doctor and nurses fussed and fidgeted for a while before they began stitching up Marcus's wound. Lucy and Shannon watched the whole procedure.

They'd been at the clinic for nearly twenty hours when Willie opened his eyes and surveyed his surroundings. He'd been unconscious most of that time and had missed a lot of the drama. Because of the copious amounts of pain medication he'd consumed, he felt better than he had for a long time. Bandages covered most of his face and his fingers were plastered together and held straight by an awkward piece of metal. He knew he was lucky to survive Jimmy and Lucy's brutality and he was grateful they hadn't done any lasting damage.

'How do you feel, sir?' Gupta asked, pulling the curtain around Willie's bed.

'Not too bad, doctor, under the circumstances.'

'Well, you've been out of it for a long time, and you need to give yourself more time to heal properly.' The doctor smiled as he checked Willie's pulse.

'Apart from the various cuts and bruises, you also have some cigarette burns. I don't know what you people were up to, but the authorities will sort it out soon enough.'

Just then, Detective Dykes appeared behind the doctor. Through the open curtain, Willie had a clear view of O'Reilly lying unconscious in the next bed with Marcus performing the last rites.

'What did you say?' Dykes asked the doctor.

'When?'

'Just now—about the authorities?'

'I have alerted the Garda in Galway, as I am required to do for gunshot wounds.'

Dykes scowled and stepped away. 'I'm a Garda detective, did I not mention that?'

'Yes sir, you did,' said Gupta, 'but I still had to report the information.'

'How is he, doctor?' Willie said, pointing at O'Reilly.

'Not good, I'm afraid. There's nothing more I can do. The bullet pierced his lung and shredded several arteries. He's lost too much blood.'

'Why didn't you get them to send a helicopter from Galway so he could get proper treatment?' Dykes shouted.

'He did get proper treatment. He couldn't be moved in the condition he was in. I had to get to work on him immediately. I consulted the specialist at the University Hospital, who concurred with my actions.'

'You consulted a specialist?' Dykes asked.

'That's correct,' Gupta said.

Willie watched as Marcus concluded the sacrament, folded his silk stole and placed it back in his pocket. Marcus realigned the sling in his arm and grimaced at the pain in his shoulder.

'The best thing we can do now is keep him comfortable,' Gupta said.

He smiled at Sarah and Lucy, who were keeping vigil. 'Can I speak to the two of you?'

Sarah and Lucy followed the doctor to the other corner of the room.

'How is Marcus, doctor?' Sarah was the first to speak.

'He's lucky. His injury is nowhere near as serious as those of the detective. The bullet seems to have gone out of its way not to do any damage.'

The doctor averted his gaze, as if he didn't know how to say what he had to say next. He looked at Lucy and frowned.

'What is it?' Lucy asked. 'I haven't got the AIDS, have I?'

'Did you know you were pregnant?'

The room went quiet as the assembled companions turned to face Lucy.

'Jaysus, the spawn of Satan on the Aran Islands,' Eamon said under his breath.

'We did a precautionary blood test before transfusing your blood into Father Nee. The results are incontrovertible.'

'How many months?' Sarah took hold of Lucy's hand to comfort her daughter.

'From the look of her, I'd say she was four and a half months gone.'

'Are there any complications? I mean, with the blood test and everything?'

'There's no way to tell from the blood. I'm sure everything is fine, but you can come in for a check-up tomorrow.'

Sarah looked at Marcus as the tears began to run down her cheeks.

'If you need me, I'll be on call all night,' the doctor said, leaving the room.

'What do we do now?' Marcus asked. 'She can't go to prison with a baby on the way.'

'It's out of my hands, Marcus,' Dykes said. 'She's broken a few laws in the last week.'

'She killed a detective,' Eamon said. 'She belongs in jail.'

'Hang on a minute,' said Dykes. 'He's not dead yet.'

'But she's just a child,' Sarah pleaded. 'She was only acting in self-defence.'

'I deserve to go to jail,' Lucy whispered. 'I caused this whole mess—if I hadn't done what I did, none of this would have happened.'

'She saved Marcus's life and stuck around to face the consequences,' said Sarah. 'She could have left Marcus there in the field to die and she could have refused to give him her blood.'

'We have more important things to consider,' Dykes said, holding the artist's sketch from the robbery.

Dykes and Marcus looked at each other and then they both stared at Willie. Dykes rose from his chair and walked to the centre of the room, keeping his eyes on Willie. He took the dark blue baseball cap out of his pocket and showed it to the Englishman. 'We have an eyewitness statement that the bank robber was wearing this cap, which we found on your boat. And they provided us with this sketch, which looks exactly like you.'

'That may be my cap,' Willie admitted, 'but it doesn't mean I robbed anything.'

'The entire Garda force in Galway will be down on top of us by morning. You better come clean.'

Willie sat up in his bed and sneered. 'I was just about to say the same thing to you.'

The fog lifted in Willie's head and the events of the past week became clear in his mind. He looked at Marcus while pointing his shattered finger at Dykes.

'This is the blackguard who robbed that bloody bank. He bought my boat and then gave me stolen money as a deposit. He gave me the dirty money that nearly got me killed.'

Dykes stood up to defend himself, his face red with anger. 'Why don't you just admit what you did?'

'Detective Dykes.' A nurse barged into the room and handed the detective a fax. 'This just came for you.'

She handed the paper to Dykes, who studied it. It was the sketch of the woman Delores had seen in her pub with the suspect.

'She looks familiar.' He stared at the sketch. He held the fax up so Marcus could see it. 'Does she look familiar to you?'

'If I didn't know any better, I'd say it looked like—' Marcus trailed off and began pacing the room.

'What the feck is going on?' Eamon barked.

Suddenly, the machines connected to O'Reilly started beeping and the doctor rushed in, followed by a squad of nurses. The doctor grabbed a syringe from the tray table and injected O'Reilly with adrenaline. The defibrillator beside the bed was charged up as the doctor grabbed the two paddles connected to it. He placed the paddles on O'Reilly's chest.

'Clear,' he shouted, watching as the electric energy coursed through the patient. He looked at the monitor above the bed and frowned.

He repeated the process several times before he placed the paddles back on the machine. Checking his watch, he turned to look at the assembled visitors. 'Time of death— eleven fifty-nine p.m.'

SUNDAY

23

DYKES stood to attention and took a deep breath. 'William Shuttleworth-Banks, Lucy Shannon and Sarah Shannon, I'm arresting you under Section 30 of the Offences against the State Act of 1939.' The words rolled off his tongue as if he were reading them from a script.

Of course, he'd said the lines so often he knew them by heart. 'You are not obliged to say anything unless you wish to do so, but whatever you say will be taken down in writing and may be given in evidence.'

'This is ridiculous,' Marcus pleaded. 'There's no way these two robbed a bloody bank.'

'Do you understand your rights as I have explained them to you?'

Willie, Lucy and Sarah nodded.

'Look, I have two eyewitness accounts that Willie paid for goods using cash that was stolen in Galway on Tuesday. I know for a fact he was in Galway at the time of the robbery because I saw him there. And now I have Miss

Shannon's likeness on an artist's sketch from one of the eyewitnesses, which puts her in the frame as well.'

Marcus picked up the artist sketches. 'But the robbery took place on Tuesday morning, and you said you didn't see Willie until Tuesday night. The artist's sketch places Sarah with Willie on Wednesday morning, twenty-four hours after the robbery. It's not even Sarah in the sketch.'

Sarah walked over to Willie's bed and held the Englishman by the hand. 'It is me in the sketch.'

'What.' Marcus couldn't believe his ears.

'We meant to tell you, Marcus, Willie and I have been—' Sarah struggled to find the correct term, '—stepping out.'

'So, you admit to stealing the money?' Dykes pressed.

'No,' Sarah shouted. 'We may have been in that pub at that time, but we didn't steal any money.'

'We were just in the wrong place at the wrong time,' Willie smiled at Sarah.

'The fact remains that you used stolen money to buy goods. I have you bang to rights.'

'But you gave me that money as a deposit on the boat,' Willie pleaded.

'That's not possible,' Dykes barked. 'That money was given to me by Detective O'Reilly. Are you suggesting Detective O'Reilly robbed the bank?'

'In the words of Sherlock Holmes, when you have eliminated the impossible, whatever remains, no matter how improbable, must be the truth,' said Willie.

Marcus sat on a chair beside O'Reilly's bed and rolled his eyes up to Heaven. 'So, you're going to keep us all here until your superiors arrive. And then you're going to tell them this cock-and-bull story?'

'Well, what else can I do?' Dykes asked. 'How else do you explain this mess? How do I explain how a detective was killed by a bullet from his own gun?'

'So, you're just going to skew the facts so these two fit in the frame?'

'I haven't skewed any facts. Just mind your own business, Father Nee. You're lucky I'm not arresting you for illegal distilling and gambling.'

Marcus was about to shout back when the door opened and in walked Judas, wagging his tail as he went.

Nobody else seemed to notice when the dog walked across the room toward O'Reilly's bed. He raised his front legs on the table containing the Garda's personal effects, using his paw to browse the items. On the table were O'Reilly's wallet, house keys, chewing gum, mobile phone and a large, ornate key that looked completely out of place. Using his paw, Judas shoved the ornate key off the table and onto the floor. Lowering his head to the floor, he picked up the key and gripped it firmly between his teeth.

'Dogs aren't allowed in here,' a nurse shouted when she saw Judas scamper toward Marcus, holding the metallic object in his mouth.

'What have you got there, Judas?' Marcus asked, reaching out to grab the key.

Marcus recognised it at once. It was the key to the tabernacle, which had been missing from the church for nearly a week.

'That's funny.' Marcus took a closer look at the key to make sure it belonged to his church.

'What's funny?' Dykes asked.

'You know what this is?' Marcus raised the key over his head to show his companions.

'Don't keep us all in suspense, dear boy!' Willie tried not to sound agitated.

'This is the key to the church tabernacle.'

'Ignoring for a moment the fact that we don't know what a tabernacle is, what's it doing among the detective's effects?' Willie asked.

'That's the million-dollar question, isn't it?' Marcus smiled. 'This key has been missing for days now, and we can't get the tabernacle open without it.'

Sensing the likelihood of a pending adventure, Willie got out of bed and searched for his clothes.

'Where do you think you're going?' Dykes rushed across the room to apprehend his suspect.

Before Willie could answer, Sarah leaped forward to block the oncoming detective's path. 'Don't come any closer, detective. You're outnumbered.'

'What are we waiting for?' Willie said, pointing in the general direction of the exit. 'To the church, I think.'

Marcus, Eamon and Lucy sneaked out of the clinic at a steady pace, keeping an eye out for the nurses as they went. When the coast was clear, they gestured for the others to follow. Willie, who was covered in bandages, Sarah and Dykes took a more circuitous route out the back door so as not to alert the medics. Alarmed at the sudden wave of humanity, Judas started barking and jumping up and down. When Lucy stopped to light a cigarette, Willie gave her a cautious look.

'Smoking will kill you, dear heart,' he whispered.

Sarah reached out her arm and grabbed the cigarette out of Lucy's mouth. 'More to the point, it will kill your baby.'

'Sorry,' Lucy whispered.

'I'm keeping my eye on the three of you,' Dykes shouted at Willie, Lucy and Sarah when they reached the centre of the village.

'Never fret, dear boy. We're not about to run for it.'

The full moon illuminated the wet road as the companions made their way past the Celtic Cross and down the *boreen* to the church. Marcus was filled with anxiety and trepidation at the thought of what might be wating for them in the tabernacle, but he knew they had to find out. As they approached the church, Marcus took another look behind him to make sure Willie was still in one piece. He climbed the steps to the main door of the church and rooted around in his pockets for the keys.

'Come on, boy. We haven't got all day,' Eamon said under his breath.

Sarah gave Eamon a playful dig in the ribs while Marcus shot his father a furious look. He managed to liberate his keys from his pocket and put the right one in the lock.

The church smelled damp as they entered. Marcus cursed under his breath at the sight of the plastic buckets strategically placed to catch the leaks from the roof.

The visitors paraded down the aisle and stopped in front of the altar to allow Marcus to genuflect. He crossed himself and carried on around the altar.

Removing the curtain from the front of the tabernacle, he placed the key in the lock. He looked around at his companions and couldn't help but smile. 'Are you ready?'

Not a peep could be heard out of anyone as Marcus turned the key. He opened the door of the tabernacle and stood back.

'That looks like O'Reilly's red duffel bag,' Dykes said as Marcus took the bag out and placed it on the altar. Pulling the two strings at the top, he opened it as wide as he could. He gasped as he looked inside. Turning the bag upside down, he emptied the contents on the altar.

Everyone looked in shock as they watched the bundles of cash falling onto the altar.

'Well, I'll be damned.' Willie leaned in to have a closer look. 'A veritable ecclesiastical ATM machine.'

'The jig is up, detective,' said Marcus. 'I think you have your bank robber.'

'Jaysus,' Eamon exclaimed. 'O'Reilly stole the money?'

'Please. This is God's house.'

'Sorry.'

They all looked at Marcus as he picked up different stacks and examined them. 'They're all in denominations of five hundred.'

'I never met Detective O'Reilly before this,' Willie reminded Dykes. 'Why were you chasing me? How did he get his hands on stolen money?'

Dykes sat down on the steps of the altar and considered the question. 'I gave it to you when I put down the deposit on your boat.'

Dykes was silent for a moment.

'O'Reilly owed me money for weeks. He gave me a thousand euro on Tuesday—two five-hundred-euro notes, just like those.' Dykes pointed at the cash on the altar.

'O'Reilly goes through Shop Street on his way to work every day. He must have seen the money outside the bank and swiped it.'

Marcus looked at Sarah and smiled. 'So, you gave the dodgy cash O'Reilly gave you to Willie, who went around town spending it. Then you followed the trail of money and ended up here—except it was you who brought the money here in the first place.'

'That's about the size of it.' Dykes sighed before continuing. 'O'Reilly was covering his tracks. He knew I was putting a deposit down on the boat that night, so he gave me some of the stolen money to use as the deposit. He thought that would send everyone in the wrong direction. He must have also destroyed the tapes from the security cameras on Shop Street so we couldn't identify him.'

'What do we do now?' Eamon asked.

'Nothing,' said Dykes. 'I will arrest Lucy for murder, attempted murder, kidnapping and assault, and return the money to its rightful owners.'

'Yes, I suppose that's the best course of action,' Eamon smiled.

'You're happy pinning the robbery on your partner and making yourself the laughing stock of the force?' Marcus asked.

'What else can I do?'

'What kind of heartless animals are you?' Sarah shouted. 'You can't send Lucy to jail with a baby on the way. She was obviously coerced into doing what she did by an older man. She's just a child—you can't let her rot away in a cell. She said she was sorry and she's willing to make amends.'

Lucy put her arm around her mother. 'It's alright, mom. They have to send me to jail. I deserve it. You can look after the baby when it's time.'

'We could keep the money and say nothing,' Willie suggested.

'We can't use the cash because the serial numbers are consecutive—we would be caught immediately,' Dykes explained.

'There are ways around that,' said Lucy.

'Aren't you in enough trouble, young lady?' Marcus asked. 'It's ludicrous to suggest we keep it.'

'It was just a suggestion,' Willie whispered.

'We can't do that,' Dykes said.

'We have to report it,' Marcus added.

'Look, I'm sorry, son,' Eamon interjected. 'I realise you have a higher purpose to serve, but the fact remains—we have all this money and no one will know if we take it.'

'It makes perfect sense, dear boy,' said Willie. 'Nobody will miss it. It's still a lot of money split five ways. You need money for your church, don't you?'

'We could say it fell off the cliff with Jimmy and scattered to the four winds,' said Willie.

'It's caused us nothing but trouble, and we should have some compensation, wouldn't you say?'

'Now, just hold on a minute,' said Marcus. 'It's not our money to keep. It's stolen money.'

'It could work out well for you, old chap,' Willie said to Dykes. 'You could take the credit for cracking the case. You say Jimmy stole the money and then accidentally scattered it over the cliff. You could go back to Galway a hero and retire on schedule—and we could keep the money.'

'That's ridiculous,' said Dykes. 'We can't just keep the money and tie everything up in a neat ribbon. I won't be able to sufficiently explain all that has happened here. O'Reilly was my responsibility, and it's my fault he was killed. My superiors will arrest me for misconduct and send me to prison. There are too many unexplained questions. Anyway, I'm being forced into retirement, and I have nothing to go back to. I don't even have a boat now.'

The companions considered the matter.

Finally, Willie smiled. 'I've got it. Sergeant Dykes can take the credit for finding the money and the thief. He can say Jimmy shot O'Reilly and Marcus before he fell over the cliff along with the money. Sarah, Lucy and I will take the yacht and bring the cash with us to Switzerland. We could then transfer the laundered funds into Marcus's church restoration account and say it came from some rich American benefactors. Marcus and Dykes can meet us next month when the dust settles.'

'A windfall from God,' said Eamon, 'to serve a higher purpose.'

'Is that okay with you, Lucy?' Marcus asked. 'You get to stay out of jail and your mother will be there to help you take care of the baby.'

'I am sorry for what I've done and I promise to make it right. It's a new start and I won't fuck it up.'

Everyone laughed.

'What do you say to that, Sarah?' Dykes asked. 'Can she be trusted to turn over a new leaf?'

'She's sorry about your partner, detective sergeant,' Sarah said as she hugged her daughter.'

'All of us will get a stipend when it's all laundered. We must allow the good Lord to transubstantiate it,' said Willie.

Marcus glared at Willie as he stuffed all the money back into the duffel bag and handed it to Dykes. 'Are we all agreed then?'

Everyone nodded.

'Sperlonga would be a nice place to bring up a child, don't you think? Willie stood bolt upright and raised his chest. 'We can go there after we finish our business in Switzerland.'

'Ah yes—your friend with the hotel,' said Marcus. 'That sounds like a nice spot to end your epic voyage. Eamon and I could visit you when I get called back to Rome.'

Sarah smiled, and everyone nodded in agreement. Marcus locked the tabernacle and ushered his companions off the altar. He made his way across the church into the sacristy and opened the back door.

24

JUDAS was waiting outside the church when the five companions came out through the back door and headed for the cove, where Willie's boat was moored. The sun was coming up, but the sky was grey and the sea was dark green, which meant that rain wasn't far off. Willie started to feel the pain as his medication wore off. He tapped Eamon on the shoulder and pointed at the Virgin Mary-shaped holy-water bottle in his back pocket. Eamon smirked and held out the bottle for Willie. They stopped for a moment as Willie drained the contents down his throat. Sarah also waited as Marcus, Lucy and Dykes carried on down the hill.

'Bless you, my son,' Willie said as he handed the bottle back.

Eamon looked at the empty bottle and glowered. 'That's the last of it, you know. There's no more to be had on the island.'

'Don't worry, old man,' Willie whispered when Marcus was out of earshot. 'I think I know where I can get my hands on some more.'

'What will I do while you go gadding around the world? Marcus will have no interest in starting a new business now that he has enough money for the church.'

'You'll just have to improvise, I suppose.'

'That's easy for you to say. I'm the one who has to stay here and see out my days in sobriety.' Eamon struggled to keep up as he followed Willie and Sarah down the hill.

'Can I go with you?' Eamon asked.

Willie turned and looked at Sarah with an expression of horror etched across his face.

'Absolutely not.'

'Why not? Sure, I'll be no trouble at all. I'll be able to help you with your bags and make you breakfast in the mornings.'

'It is solitude and quietness I crave, old boy. Anyway, I'm sure Marcus would be heartbroken to see you go.'

'He would not. He'd be glad to see the back of me.'

'That's as maybe, but I'm afraid we can't fit you in. The old tub only sleeps three.'

'I'll have my own money, of course. Don't worry on that score,' Eamon pleaded as they caught up to Marcus.

'Your own money for what?' Marcus asked.

'Am I not entitled to a share of the booty?'

'I thought you were donating it to the church fund?'

'What gave you that impression?'

'I suppose I just thought you had considered the consequences of not donating to the church fund.'

'What consequences are those?'

'Well now, let's see. I would disown you, for starters. You would have nobody to cook and clean for you, and you would be all alone for the rest of your life.'

'No, I wouldn't. Sure, I have plenty of friends.'

'Not after I put it around that you destroyed Willie's still and made sure there was no more booze for anyone.'

'You wouldn't do that.'

'Try me.' Marcus smiled as he saw the expression on his father's face. 'You know I don't begrudge you the money, but it's for the greater good, and for your health.'

Marcus put his free arm on his father's shoulder and gave him a consolatory smile.

'Will Detective O'Reilly get the full honours at the funeral?' Marcus asked Dykes, who was still carrying the red duffel bag.

'I don't see why not. As far as my superiors know, he is a hero. He lost his life in the line of duty and stopped the money falling into the wrong hands.'

'I might go along myself. I'll say a prayer for all of us,' Marcus said.

'I'm sure he'd appreciate that.'

Marcus turned to Willie and noticed that he and Sarah were holding hands. They looked embarrassed and let go of each other's hands.

'You make a nice couple,' said Marcus.

Willie nodded and kissed Sarah on the cheek.

'I never got a chance to say congratulations before,' Marcus said as he gave Sarah a peck on the cheek. 'I'm happy for you both, if not a little surprised.'

'Guilty as charged,' Sarah laughed.

Marcus slapped Willie on the back. 'And now we know why you wanted to go on a little voyage. Now, you take care of her, or you'll have me to answer to.'

When they reached the beach, the companions looked across the harbour and marvelled at the morning drama unfolding at the pier.

II

Sergeant Seamus Gilligan had never seen the harbour so busy, even at the height of the holiday season. Just an hour before, he'd been tucked up in bed when he got the call from Galway saying a dozen guards were on their way. He was to arrange transport, they'd said—something about stolen money and dead detectives. Whatever it was, he was sure it would end in tears.

He watched as the uniformed guards jumped out of the trawler and landed on the pier, bowing his head when the Special Branch detectives, led by Superintendent Frank Delaney, took their turns jumping onto the dock.

Without being told, the guards climbed into the waiting jaunting cars and awaited their orders.

Gilligan, wearing his full-dress uniform, complete with shiny belt buckle and buttons, looked out of place next to the other officers.

'Are you Gilligan?' Delaney asked, climbing onto the leading car.

'Yes, sir,' Gilligan stammered. 'Yes sir, I am.'

'Take us to Dykes—on the double.'

'Don't you want a cuppa tea first? We have sandwiches laid on up at the pub. You must have a terrible thirst on you after the trip.'

'Take us to Dykes or I'll have you shot. I'm already holding you personally responsible for losing the money and getting one of our men killed.'

Gilligan leaned on one of the jaunting cars and looked out onto the ocean in despair.

'Why are you all dolled up?' Delaney asked.

Gilligan nearly fell over when the jaunting car on which he was leaning started its slow journey along the pier and into the village. He doubled back and retrieved his dilapidated black bicycle. Mounting the contraption, he rode as fast as he could in the direction of the clinic, averting his gaze when he passed the jaunting cars. When he reached the clinic, he ditched the bicycle and ran inside the building, shouting for the doctor.

III

Willie, Lucy and Sarah climbed aboard the yacht and began the preparations to put to sea. Willie raised the anchor and checked the fuel gauge before he climbed the steps to the wheelhouse and started the engine. Climbing back down, he went aft to help Sarah with the anchor.

'We have plenty of fuel for France, dear boy,' Willie announced, cleaning his hands in the clear sea water. He reached into a secret compartment at the side of the yacht and fished out two bottles of poteen. He threw them on the sandy beach in the general vicinity of Eamon.

'Don't say I never give you anything.'

Judas barked as Willie leaned over the side and shook hands with Marcus and Eamon.

'We'll make our way to Cannes and wait for you and Dykes to join us in Zurich in a week or so. Then it's off to the Italian Riviera. I'll send you the details.'

Marcus, Dykes and Eamon watched as Willie cast off and the yacht made its way out of the cove.

'Bon voyage,' Marcus called as he caught a glimpse of the guards in the village. 'We have a lot of explaining to do.'

'I'll buy you a drink if we ever get away with this,' Dykes laughed.

'Do you think we can trust him?' Eamon whispered to Marcus.

Marcus looked at his father. 'If you can't trust an Englishman, who can you trust?'

They stood on the beach as the boat's diesel engine roared away. They had a clear view of Kilronan village, where the guards were making their way to the clinic.

'Alright, we better get a move on before they start arresting people,' said Dykes.

Finally, they turned around and made their way off the beach. Marcus turned and saw that the boat was a good distance away. Sarah, Lucy and Willie were still standing side by side waving. Marcus noticed Judas by his side and was about to shout at him until he saw the triumphant look on the dog's face. Then he saw the impressive pile of shit he had just excreted.

'Well done, boy,' Marcus said as he petted the dog's head, 'better late than never.'

EPILOGUE

SUPERINTENDENT Frank Delaney stubbed his cigarette out in the ashtray and looked at Marcus and Dykes.

They were sitting in Sergeant Gilligan's office at the Kilronan Garda Station, going over the events of the past week. The only other person in the office was Garda Duignan, who was transcribing Marcus's version of events onto his laptop.

'So, this Jimmy Roberts character stole the money in Galway and made his way to the Aran Islands with his reluctant accomplice, Lucy Shannon.'

Marcus and Dykes had already synchronised their recollection of the week's events to get their story straight for the debriefing with Delaney. They were careful to leave out any details that would implicate O'Reilly and Lucy, more importantly, land themselves in jail as accomplices. They were buoyed by the fact that their watered-down version of events was more plausible than what actually happened. By placing the blame for the whole sorry affair at the feet of Jimmy, who wasn't alive to contradict their version, they were confident they could fool a man even of Delaney's cynicism and lack of trust.

'That's correct,' said Marcus.

'Detective Sergeant Dykes apprehended Roberts after he shot you and O'Reilly with the gun he had already stolen from Dykes.'

'Yes.'

'And Roberts somehow fell over a cliff along with the money as Dykes was trying to arrest him.'

'Yes. But he recovered the guns.'

'And what about William Shuttleworth-Banks and Sarah Shannon?'

'We interrogated them at length, sir,' said Dykes. 'We felt confident about removing them from our inquiries.'

'You felt confident about this despite this sketch provided by a witness,' Delaney said, holding up the likeness of Sarah.

'We were able to ascertain that that was, in fact, a sketch of Lucy, who bears a striking resemblance to her mother.'

'Very striking, I'd say.' Delaney turned to Marcus. 'How did you and Shuttleworth-Banks end up wounded if you weren't involved?'

'They were caught in the crossfire, sir,' Dykes jumped in. 'We apprehended Roberts quite close to Nees' farm, and the pair of them was in the vicinity at the time.'

Delaney held up a sheet of paper in front of Dykes. 'You know what this is, don't you?'

Dykes pretended not to know.

'This entitles you to an honourable retirement with a full pension. If I believed that load of bollocks you're after telling me and signed this piece of paper, you'd be a free man.'

'Yes, sir.'

The door opened. Sergeant Gilligan entered with a tray of tea and Jacob's Cream Crackers.

Delaney frowned. 'Could you not get any proper biscuits?' he barked. 'These are no good without butter. Could you not get any butter?'

'Cutbacks, sir,' said Gilligan.

Delaney leaned back in his chair while keeping an eye on Gilligan.

'Gilligan,' he cleared his throat, 'this Eamon Nee character who was arrested along with Detective O'Reilly—is he related to Father Nee here?'

'Yes, sir. He's his father.'

'And Lucy Shannon—she stole a bicycle the other day before her mother and Father Nee stole bicycles and chased after her. What was that all about?'

Gilligan sat down and used a towel to wipe the sweat from his forehead.

'That was just a domestic dispute, sir. Father Marcus is an old friend of the family. The bicycles and the damage have already been paid for, so no charges were brought.' Gilligan paused to wipe more sweat off his brow. 'Lucy Shannon was taken against her will while pregnant. There are also psychological issues. She hadn't been taking her medication, so she wasn't the full shilling. With the proper medicine, she'll be fine.'

Delaney gestured for Gilligan to leave, and then he asked Duignan to read the statement back to him. When that was done, Duignan printed out the statement for Marcus to sign. Delaney stared at Marcus for what seemed like an eternity. He picked up his pen.

'You see this pen? This pen was once used by Charles J. Haughey, our beloved former Taoiseach. And now you're going to use it to endorse a pack of lies.'

'The pen should be used to it, so,' Duignan laughed.

Delaney ignore the comment and handed the pen to Marcus, who signed the statement.

'I want your warrant card and your weapon,' Delaney said to Dykes.

When Dykes handed the items over, Delaney presented him with his retirement document.

'Signed, sealed and delivered,' said Delaney. 'Enjoy your retirement.'

'Thank you, sir.' Dykes looked at the letter and placed it in his inside jacket pocket.

'I think, under the circumstances, you should not come back to the mainland for a while. I'm going to have a hell of a time selling this nonsense to the Assistant Commissioner of Internal Affairs with you under foot.'

'That's fair enough, boss.'

'It means you'll miss the funeral, of course.'

Dykes rummaged through his pockets, located his car keys and fiddled with them for a moment. He then placed a metal object on the desk in front of Delaney.

Delaney picked up the object and looked at it. It was a gold medal in the shape of a Celtic cross, with the words 'Scott Medal—For Valor' written on one side.

'I'd be grateful if you'd put that in O'Reilly's coffin before the funeral. He was killed trying to save my life.'

II

Dykes was standing near the altar, staring at the tabernacle, when Marcus and Eamon joined him.

'That's the trouble with those things,' said Marcus. 'You have to watch them every second.'

Dykes laughed and turned to shake hands with Marcus. He was taken aback by the strange, hairy object in the priest's hand. 'What's that when it's at home?'

'This is a toupee,' Marcus explained. 'It was handed in by one of my parishioners as evidence that someone is robbing his chickens.'

'Sounds like a crime wave,' said Dykes. 'Do you need me to investigate?'

'You're retired now, remember? Anyway, I know who the culprit is. I just have to unmask his accomplices. A little hell fire and brimstone should do the trick.'

Eamon tried to avoid making eye contact with his son by staring at the ground.

'And you thought they would benefit from spiritual enlightenment? Or was it enlightened spirits?'

'Here, I have a retirement present for you,' said Marcus, handing Dykes a pen. 'This used to belong to our beloved former Taoiseach.'

Dykes laughed as he accepted the gift.

'You're a crafty rogue, you know that?'

'He called me a liar—he won't get away with that.'

'So, you'll be here for a while then?' Eamon asked Dykes.

'That's about the size of it.'

'You wouldn't be interested in a spot of roofing, would you,' Marcus asked, 'when the weather gets better?'

They laughed as they walked back down the aisle, avoiding the plastic buckets as they went.

The End

ACKNOWLEDGMENTS

I appreciate the collaborative efforts of the editors (Tom Power and Richard Weavers), the cover designer (ebooklaunch.com) and my family (in order of appearance, Donal, Eileen, Maeve, Geraldine Ann, Fintan, Derek, Jan and Cáit). I am grateful to Alan Caulfield for coming up with the idea for the Virgin Mary holy-water bottles.

AUTHOR'S NOTE

'Dirty Old Town' was written by Ewan MacColl. The Sherlock Holmes quote was written by Arthur Conan Doyle.

CONTACT THE AUTHOR

Twitter: Ronan Joyce@ronan_joyce
Facebook: http://facebook.com/ronan.joyce
LinkedIn: linkedin.com/in/ronan-joyce-1352b0144/
Email: ronan.joyce@hotmail.com
Website: ronanjoyce.com

Please check out my other books…

HOLLYWOOD HOODLUMS

Adam and Nigel are desperate to rekindle the fame and fortune they enjoyed in the eighties with a hit song they could never replicate. When their friend Archie writes a screenplay about their brief brush with success, they embark on an unorthodox mission to get it made into a movie. Discouraged by the chilly reception they receive in Hollywood, they meet a scheming rogue who concocts a dangerous plan that promises to get them back on the road to stardom. Luckily for Adam and Nigel, love has a way of thwarting even the best-laid plans.

NEE-JERK REACTION (MARCUS NEE VOL. II)

Monsignor Marcus Nee makes a chilling discovery when his student steals a vintage Mercedes-Benz that once belonged to Rudolf Hess. He finds, hidden in the car, a shocking letter written by Adolf Hitler that will have devastating implications if it ever sees the light of day. With neo-Nazi thugs, MI-6 agents and Interpol officers in hot pursuit, Marcus sets out on a deadly quest to save his friends and prevent his terrifying secret from falling into the wrong hands. He must put his life on the line and confront his demons if he is to deliver his comrades from evil.

An excerpt from *Nee-Jerk Reaction* follows. Please enjoy.

NEE-JERK REACTION

CHAPTER ONE

Augsburg-Haunstetten, Germany, 1941

AS THE oversized Mercedes-Benz 770 limousine lumbered toward the air base, the man in the back seat sat uncomfortably in his opulent surroundings. He seldom made a fuss about such matters but the delicacy of the mission at hand underlined the importance of being seen in a vehicle befitting his status in the Third Reich. He eyed the velvet seats and plush carpet and was glad he had cleaned his boots before he climbed inside.

The varnished mahogany panels all around glistened in the sun and he could see his reflection in the polished chrome of the door and window handles. He looked resplendent in his leather Luftwaffe flying suit with the second-class Iron Cross he had won in the Great War hanging below his neck. His closely cropped dark hair, thick bushy eyebrows, and long straight nose blended in nicely with his German face.

He opened the drinks cabinet between the two opposite seats and was surprised to see bottles of the finest Cognacs, brandies, whiskies, schnapps and vodkas. A set of Waterford Crystal glasses, a gift from Joseph Kennedy, the U.S. ambassador to Britain, sat on a shelf of its own lined with velvet padding. Opening a mirrored compartment, he found a box of Upmann's cigars and premium Swiss chocolates. He was relieved to see, amid the unnecessary clutter, a simple bottle of Bavarian still water. He picked up the bottle, opened it, and poured some of the liquid into one of the crystal glasses. He took a small glass jar out of his briefcase and placed two homeopathic pellets from the jar into the water. Picking up the glass, he placed it to his lips and swallowed the contents, pellets and all.

He had long since taken to consuming his homeopathic remedies in private, such was the vitriolic criticism it prompted from his colleagues. He was horrified that his preoccupation with his health and his unorthodox treatment regimen should be such a bone of contention during his visits to the Berghof.

The road to the air base was lined by squadrons of infantry soldiers who stood to attention and saluted as the car swished past. Even if the size and magnificence of the vehicle had not alerted them to the importance of its occupant, they were forewarned by the red banner that hung from the silver flag pole on the right front wing of the car. It bore a white eagle and swastika inside a black circle—the insignia of the Deputy Führer.

Anxious to hold on to what little power he had left in the Reich, Rudolf Hess took every opportunity to display the trappings of his office. Even if this mission required him to wear a flying suit bearing the rank of a Luftwaffe captain, he was determined to show as few signs as possible of his diminishing status. Over the flying suit, he wore a tunic bearing the insignia of his true rank. He also made sure the uniforms of his staff bore ranks appropriate to their stations.

Erich Sommer, his driver and bodyguard, wore the uniform of a Luftwaffe major, and Karlheinz Pintsch, Hess's adjutant, wore the uniform of a Luftwaffe colonel. Of course, those were only the ranks that they were displaying for this mission; in reality, they were both SS officers of the Gestapo. Both men had been loyal servants since 1933, when Hess had been appointed Deputy Führer, following Hitler's elevation to Reich Chancellor. They had been career officers in the Prussian Secret Police with special duties to protect government officials. They became SS officers in 1936 when Hitler unified all German police forces into the Gestapo. They appeared rugged and daunting, but Hess had no doubts about their loyalty. Their duties often brought them to Hess's private home and they always showed his wife, Ilse, and his son, Wolf, the utmost respect. He knew that both men would lay down their lives for his and that they would protect his family during his absence.

Hess flipped open a mahogany table attached to the door and marvelled at the exquisite craftsmanship and the superior German design. He took a small leather-bound journal out of his briefcase and placed it on the table. The journal was worn with age but the swastika was still prominent on the front cover. As he shuffled through the book, taking care not to dislodge any of the fragile pages, he considered the names that caught his eye and recounted the events that had brought him to this point in his life. It had been Hess's idea to travel to Britain and negotiate a deal with King George VI to keep Britain out of the war. The Führer had been sceptical at first, but Hess had convinced him that the imminent invasion of Russia would make the prospect of fighting the war on two fronts more likely.

The Deputy Führer had begun formulating the plan six months before with his friend Albrecht Haushofer, who had been acquainted with Douglas Douglas-Hamilton, the Duke of Hamilton. Hess had arranged to meet Prince George, the Duke of Kent, at Hamilton's estate in Scotland to get him to convince his brother, King George VI, to end Britain's involvement in the war. He believed that the British establishment had no desire to be involved in the conflict in Europe and that their only real concern was the protection of their dominions and territories around the world. Thanks to his conversations with the overbearing Ambassador Kennedy, Hess knew the United States had no intention of entering the war. Through a series of clandestine intermediaries and secret missives, he had reasoned that Britain could never hope to beat the might of Germany, especially with a drunkard like Winston Churchill at the helm. And without the United States, Britain was on its own. After all, the British royal family were themselves of German stock and should have no wish to get in the way of the Nazi desire for Lebensraum.

Hess had to admit a certain delight at the thought that his brainchild had the potential to put him back in favour; he had long since been frustrated at being pushed out of Hitler's inner circle by his disagreeable counterparts Hermann Göring and Martin Bormann. The Deputy Führer had always been motivated by his loyalty to Hitler and a desire to be useful to him; however, he had been forced to concede that only through the accumulation of power could he take advantage of his position and keep his place by the Führer's side. But he understood that, should the plan fail, the Führer would deny all knowledge of the mission and dismiss Hess as a madman. This was of great concern to Hess, who was aware there was a chance he would not secure a peace deal and make a triumphant return as a hero of the Third Reich. He had to protect his good name and the good name of his father.

Reaching into the inside pocket of his tunic, Hess removed a letter bearing the official red wax seal of the Führer himself. He opened the letter, which he had received only a few hours before, and read it for the hundredth time. Glancing at the signature written on the bottom of the typed letter, he noted with pride the unmistakable hand of Adolf Hitler. He was convinced the letter, which carried as it did the best wishes of the Führer, would serve as a fitting testament that he was not a madman who disobeyed orders to embark on a fool's errand. It also carried assurances from Hitler that, upon his safe return to Germany, he would be reinstated as the Führer's immediate successor. Closing the letter, he placed it between the pages of the journal. He made no attempt to hide the forlorn expression on his face as the Mercedes turned into the busy airfield. *God protect me as I do what must be done.*

The car made its way between agitated soldiers as they loaded various planes and trucks with cargo. No matter how busy they were, protocol dictated that they stand to attention and salute when Hess's car passed. It stopped alongside a Messerschmitt 110 fighter plane parked just off the runway. Pintsch got out of the passenger seat and tried to open the back door.

'Give me a moment, will you?'

'Of course, Herr Reich Minister,' Pintsch said as he walked away from the car to give his boss some privacy.

Hess closed the journal, snapped its fastener, and locked it. He placed the key on the seat beside him and reached down to place the journal by his feet. 'Remind me of the sequence, Sommer,' Hess said as he looked up at the driver.

Without looking at his boss, Sommer recited the combination of the secret compartment under the floor. 'Raise the armrest on the left-hand side and lift up the seat slightly.'

Hess did as he was instructed and waited for the click.

The previous day, when he had taken possession of the car at the Reich's Chancellery in Berlin, Sommer had taken the precaution of having the secret compartment fitted by a discreet furniture maker of his acquaintance. He had taken the same precaution for all the vehicles his boss had used during his time as Deputy Führer. The furniture maker had spent all night on the job and ended up with a mechanical hideaway that was undetectable to anyone who didn't know it was there.

Hess pulled away the carpet and groped around the floorboards for the latch. He opened the secret compartment and placed the journal inside. He closed the compartment and replaced the carpet, straightening his uniform as he looked ahead. He grabbed the key and handed it to Sommer, who was still sitting in the driver's seat. The two men looked at each other for a moment, as if to acknowledge a secret pact to which they alone were privy. Hess patted the young officer on the shoulder and smiled. 'Guard this with your life, Sommer. If I am not back in three days, you know what to do.'

Sommer placed the key in his uniform pocket. Hess got out of the car and smiled at his adjutant. He took another letter out of his tunic pocket and handed it to Pintsch.

'See that this is delivered after I take off.'

Pintsch accepted the letter, which was addressed to Hitler, and stood to attention. He said, 'The world will remember your actions today, Herr Reich Minister. The lives of millions are in your hands.'

Hess made an about-turn and walked towards the plane, eyeing the craft up and down as he went. He returned the 'Heil Hitler' salute of a nearby flight mechanic and kneeled to inspect the wheels.

Hess had trained on the two-seater twin-engine aircraft for about seven months under the watchful eye of Wilhelm Stör, the chief test pilot at Messerschmitt, and his colleague, Helmut Kaden. He had logged many cross-country flights and felt confident he could complete the task at hand. With a smile on his face, he remembered Hitler's idea to publicly prohibit him from flying so that he could later disavow all knowledge of Hess's actions. It took him a while, but he found a loyal ground crew that was willing to turn a blind eye to his activities and keep the mission a secret. He had chosen his favourite plane and had it modified to include a radio compass, oxygen delivery system and long-range fuel tanks.

Hess considered it ironic that his nemesis, Hermann Göring, was a proponent of the Messerschmitt Bf 110. It was developed in the 1930s and was intended for use by the Luftwaffe during the war. It would normally be armed with two MG FF 20 mm cannons, four 7.92 mm MG 17 machine guns and one 7.92 mm MG 15 machine gun, but Hess had these weapons removed to make the plane lighter. After all, this was supposed to be a mission of peace, not war. The Bf 110's lack of agility in the air was a weakness that Hess considered irrelevant considering the current mission.

Colonel Kurt Schmidt, the chief of the Met Office, sauntered out of his hut, followed by Kaden and Willy Messerschmitt himself.

'Greetings, Herr Hess,' said Messerschmitt. To the annoyance of high-ranking Nazis, the renowned aircraft engineer and designer always made a point of avoiding references to military or political rank.

Hess opted to disregard the slight and shook the designer's hand with a smile. He also shook hands with Kaden and thanked him for being so patient during his many hours of training. All three men looked up at the plane and admired her lean design.

They turned their attention to Schmidt when the colonel coughed and tapped his chest with his clipboard for dramatic effect. Hess did not like the look on the colonel's face—he couldn't bear another cancellation and braced for the worst. The flight had been postponed several times already due to mechanical problems and inclement weather, but Hess was determined that today was the day. Tonight would be a full moon, and his astrology charts showed that the planets were uniquely aligned for an immediate departure.

Schmidt looked at his notes and said, 'Outbreaks of rain or drizzle are expected over the North Sea and will become persistent, and sometimes heavy, in coastal districts along the northeast of Great Britain...'.

That doesn't sound so bad, Hess thought, as he allowed a smile to cross his face.

'Patches of fog will affect the coast of Scotland. Otherwise mainly dry, with early patches of mist and drizzle largely dying out, allowing some bright, or short sunny intervals, to develop locally. Lowest temperatures seven to ten Celsius, with moderate to fresh southerly breezes.'

Hess waited for a moment for the colonel to continue, but then he could wait no longer. 'So, am I cleared for take-off?'

'Yes, Herr Reich Minister, you are cleared for take-off.'

Hess raised his arm and punched the air with his fist. He allowed himself a triumphant smile and gestured to Sommer to join him. He took off his tunic and handed it to the driver. Kaden and Messerschmitt clapped their hands in unison but it was unclear if they were happy for Hess or if they were just glad their part in his secret mission was at an end.

'The time has come, gentlemen,' Hess said as he placed his hands on the rails at the side of the aircraft and climbed toward the cockpit.

The assembled onlookers watched in horror as Hess slipped on the first footrest and banged his knee on the aircraft. They waited as the senior Nazi grabbed hold of the rails again and made a second attempt to reach the cockpit. Everyone breathed a sigh of relief when Hess finally made it to his seat in the cockpit and began the pre-flight check.

'You carry with you the hopes of the Reich, Herr Reich Minister,' said Sommer, handing Hess a bag of supplies.

With a final check of the instrument panel, Hess switched on the ignition and tested the wing flaps. After the mechanics removed the wheel blocks, he eased the aircraft away from the building. He guided it across the air base and settled at the near end of the runway. At fourteen minutes to six on the evening of May 10, Hess applied full throttle and began his take-off run. Over a dozen people watched as the fighter plane ascended and disappeared into the sun.

www.ingramcontent.com/pod-product-compliance
Lightning Source LLC
Chambersburg PA
CBHW021029130626
46552CB00005B/1745